# ZINNIA'S SOLSTICE DADDY

## HOLIDAY DADDY DOMS
### BOOK FOUR

## RAISA GREYWOOD

Cover art by Wicked Smart Designs.
Editing provided by Briggs Consulting LLC and A Book A Day Author Services.

Ebook ISBN: 978-1-952596-34-6
Print ISBN: 978-1-952596-35-3

# PROLOGUE

*Serena* followed the line of soldiers, keeping an eye on Mitchell Sakurai. As usual, he was in the front, too dominant and protective to give up the most dangerous position.

Armored clothing the color of the surrounding mountains covered him from head to toe, hiding his lean body. The face shield on his helmet revealed a hint of the thick black beard he'd grown but concealed his remarkable light brown eyes.

If she had to pick a favorite out of all the dominants she'd helped to educate, it would have been Mitchell. A master rigger even before coming to her for lessons, he was quiet and reserved, yet had a dry wit she enjoyed. She'd never tell a soul, but he was the only one with whom she'd developed a relationship beyond that of teacher and student. He'd become a friend, and the only person she trusted to give her advice about managing her dear Lucia's little.

Of course, now that Lucia and Ryan had each other, she could move on to helping Mitchell.

Gabriel, her boss, and the angel she loved to hate, had demanded she not interfere with Mitchell beyond what was necessary to keep him alive. However, she might or might not have told him a slight fib. Although she wanted to keep Mitchell breathing and safe, she also wanted to help him find that special little girl who would complete him. He never played with the same sub twice, meaning his relationships were shallow and temporary at best. It was irritating to a woman who wanted a happily ever after for everyone.

"Testosterone poisoning," Lucifer muttered, taking her arm to help her over a chunk of fallen rock. "Traipsing through these mountains wanting to be heroes."

"I thought you'd be happy with this location. All this war must be filling Hell with souls quite nicely."

"Bah." His face reddened and he scowled. "You'd be surprised at how few there are."

"Oh? Why did you come, then?"

She hurried forward, her Manolo pumps gliding over loose rock and scree. All these mountains filled with blind spots and caves made her nervous for Mitchell, and the fiercely biting wind made it impossible to hear anything. She didn't have time to focus on her unwanted companion.

"Is it so impossible to believe it's for your charming company?" he countered.

"Considering I offered to lock you in male chastity the last time we spoke, yes, I'm afraid it is."

"So distrustful." He was suddenly at her back and pulled her to a stop, his arms wrapped loosely around her hips. "I simply wanted to see what you find so attractive about this unpleasant duty."

"We've discussed this before," she murmured. It did no good to wriggle free. He'd simply come back like a bad penny. It was an utter shame she liked it. Lucifer made her feel... Well, like there was someone out there who understood her. Her brand of love wasn't kind or gentle. She wanted rough and dirty, and she wanted to hurt people.

And sometimes, she wanted to see them bleed for it.

She never revealed herself, knowing her kinks went beyond appropriate levels of safe and sane. Yet

Lucifer accepted those darker desires and welcomed them.

It didn't help she wanted him badly. Thankfully, neither of them was willing to compromise, so there was no hope of anything happening between them.

If it ever did, they'd set the cosmos on fire.

"I want Mitchell to be safe and find happiness."

"I didn't realize you harbored such altruism."

"Hardly. Sadistic dominatrix, remember?"

He grunted and let her pull away to follow the line of soldiers. "Yet you're still out here following cannon fodder into an ambush."

"What?" Horrified, she spun to face him. "Where?"

There was no way she could protect all of Mitchell's men. To do so would mean revealing her presence, and she'd promised Gabriel she wouldn't break any of the new guardian commandments they'd hammered out. She wouldn't be able to protect Mitchell either, considering he'd be the first in the line of fire.

Lucifer lifted a negligent hand. "About half a mile ahead. Not far now." Stepping closer, he drew a claw over the curve of her jaw. "I might be willing to help you keep them safe though."

"Thank you," she breathed. "Can we turn them around somehow? What do we need to do?"

"All you have to do is accept a gift from me, lovely angel. I have in my possession the men who shot all those women and children in that Kabul maternity hospital. I will gift them to you. They will receive the punishment they deserve at your expert hands, and Mitchell will remain alive and able to find the true love you so want for him."

Serena should have known better. Lucifer never gave anything away for free. Still, unfettered access to the men who had committed the horrifying crime against humanity was very tempting. Thinking of all the things she'd do to them made her heart beat faster with cruel anticipation.

There was no such thing as a safe word in Hell.

"In exchange for what?"

"Such a simple thing," he murmured, brushing his lips over hers. "Kneel for me, darling. Accept this as your last assignment as a guardian angel and agree I will forever be your lord and master."

"Did you set this up?" she asked, wanting to strangle him. "Did you arrange for Mitchell to walk into a trap?"

"No, but I probably would have if I'd thought to do so." He dug a claw into the tender skin just under

5

her chin, forcing her to lift her head. "They're almost in range," he murmured. "Tick tock, Serena."

"I… I can't just—"

"As a bonus to celebrate our new relationship, I'll even throw in the rescue of Zinnia Ann Turner. She was abducted about a year ago and is imprisoned in a tiny cave just ahead. In fact, Mitchell is almost on top of her."

"What? Why is she there?"

"They took her to provide medical care, although I fail to see how a Doctors Without Borders midwife is going to help them unless they can suddenly give birth." He let go of her chin, allowing her to step back. "She's unmarried, and an appropriate age. She and Mitchell would suit, considering they both have that unfortunate hero complex."

"Is she… unharmed?"

"So far, yes, but I doubt that will remain true forever." He glanced over her head and smirked. "Did I just hear the sound of a gun being cocked?"

Letting out a breath, Serena sank to her knees for the first time in her life.

# CHAPTER 1

Mitch lifted a spotting scope, hoping to get a glimpse ahead. His Spidey senses were tingling, both from the uncanny wind and the dust haze obscuring his vision. "Are we sure about your informant's tip?"

"As sure as I can be, sir."

"I just don't see how an American woman would still be alive after all this time. She's already been declared dead."

Zinnia Ann Turner had been a beautiful woman with dark hair and mahogany skin kissed with gold. She'd been barely twenty-seven with a brilliant future ahead of her. Despite being missing for over a year and presumed dead, Mitch still carried her photograph. He'd been fascinated with her since the moment his friend Kaden mentioned he still harbored hope of finding her. The chances of her being alive were a million to one, but it was a reminder of why he was here and what he fought against. He never wanted to see another woman lose her life like that.

Hell, he still stalked her social media memorial page. It was probably strange to be so fascinated with a woman who was most likely dead, but he couldn't seem to help himself.

This mission was his last chance to find her. The entire base was about to be shipped home. At forty-two, he'd spent over half his life in the Army, and it would soon be time to retire. He wanted to settle down, find a little girl of his own like his best friends, Kaden, Tennyson, and Ryan had done, and maybe get a dog. Not necessarily in that order.

Then again, at his age, finding a little girl wasn't going to be as easy as it might have been for his friends.

"It probably isn't Zinnia, sir, but if there's a chance some other woman is here..." Corporal Jason Mendez shrugged. "We have to try."

"Yeah."

Moving into the point position, Mitch waved his

men back, the silent command obeyed without question. He said a prayer to anyone who might be listening—in both his Christian mother's and his Buddhist father's faiths—in a desperate hope for the wind to quiet itself to a low roar and let the dust settle.

Without warning, the wind simply stopped, leaving him frozen in shock for a split second. Brilliant sunlight illuminated the crags and cliffs of the foothills, revealing dozens of armed men in black arrayed less than a hundred yards in front of them.

From behind him, one of his men shouted, "Twelve o'clock! Target at twelve!"

The pop and whoosh of a mortar spurred him into action. Cursing, he dove to the side, then looked back to see if his men had similarly avoided the deadly shell.

From his right, Private Carter Pritchard laid down covering fire from his perch behind a boulder. Two men fell, then a third, their dying cries echoing. Returning fire, the enemy closed the distance, obviously sure their greater numbers would prevail.

"Dumbasses," Carter muttered, slapping another magazine into his rifle. "Fish in a fucking barrel."

"The mortar first," Mitch ordered. "Then you can have fun."

"Yes, sir. I'm going to have words with Mendez's informant. He led us into an ambush." Lifting the rifle, he took careful aim and fired, removing both men who had been aiming the artillery.

Grimacing, Mitch picked off two combatants who had been trying to flank them. He and his unit had been an easy target. Just a whispered mention of an American woman being held hostage had sent them running. It wouldn't be Zinnia, but one woman brought to safety and sent home would make everything they did mean something.

Lifting his head, Carter pointed. "We've got a runner at ten—"

"No, we don't." Mitch took aim and fired, dropping the last combatant in his tracks.

"Nice shooting, Tex."

Instead of answering, he gave the command to fan out for survivors. He didn't want to miss a single one. Lifting his spotting scope, he scanned the area, but saw no immediate signs of life. A flash of red caught his attention, but disappeared before he could focus.

Odd, it looked like a woman's dress shoe.

Shaking away the perplexing image, he eased around the boulder he'd been hiding behind and stayed low as he crept toward the dead combatants. Now was not the time to lose concentration.

"Colonel!"

The shout came too late, and the sudden punch of a bullet hitting his body armor knocked him backward. Silhouetted against the sun, a man stood and lifted a rifle to his shoulder, setting up another shot.

Bullets screamed over his head from all directions, riddling the man's body until he collapsed in an unmoving heap.

"You okay there, sir?" Marcus Jones asked, his freckled face creased with concern.

"I'm good." Mitch touched his ribs, wincing at the sore spot. He'd have a hell of a bruise in the morning. "Any casualties?"

"Nope. Think we got them all."

"Good." He took the hand Marcus offered and stood. "Stay alert. We probably won't find anything, but it won't hurt to look for what we came to find."

"Think there's a woman here?" Carter asked.

"No," Jason said, scowling. "We got our asses set up."

"Not your fault, Corporal. It's happened to all of us," Mitch replied. "But we'll still look."

"We have an hour until dusk," Marcus said. "Not much time."

"Ten minutes," Mitch replied, knowing he couldn't put his men at risk for a lost cause any longer. "After that, we bug out."

ZINNIA WAS ABSOLUTELY positive she heard English. After so much time hearing and speaking nothing but Dari, her ears ached for the sound of her native language.

Of course, she heard loads of gunfire too, but that was normal, and she didn't pay it much notice until it stopped completely.

What she couldn't ignore was the chain around her ankle. She supposed it was better than the alternative though. Her captors had threatened to smash her feet with a hammer if she tried to run again. She might be malnourished, filthy, and have a couple of loose teeth, but if this was a rescue, she'd be able to walk out of here under her own steam.

At least they hadn't touched her, aside from a few slaps here and there, thanks to the cheap wedding ring she always wore while on assignment. Even her escape attempts had been somewhat tolerated at first because the men who held her thought she'd been trying to return to a husband.

Aside from a small hole in the ceiling of her cave, the only exit was a steel door mounted into the stone, locked and barred against escape. Even if she managed to get past the door, the cave system was riddled with unlit passages she had no hope of navigating without a map and a light source.

Didn't mean she hadn't tried.

She crossed her fingers and sent up a prayer. Judging by her probably incorrect calculations, it was Ostara. If there was one person on this planet who needed a joyous equinox, it was Zinnia Ann Turner.

Crawling to the bottle of cloudy water her captors had given her, she took a deep swallow and grimaced at the taste of iron, hoping she had enough air in her lungs to do what needed to be done.

She lifted herself as high as she could toward the single pinpoint of light marking the opening to her cave, then willed her voice to rise up and be heard.

"If you're American, help me!" she screamed. "Canadian or British works too!"

Dead silence met her words.

Biting back a sob, she tried again, her voice

weaker, but no less needful. "Français? Deutsch? Español? Italiano?"

*Goddess, please let them hear.*

"Help me, please!"

"Ma'am, say something!" a male voice shouted, thankfully in English. "Tell us where you are!"

The tears came, full-blown sobs that stole her breath. "Down here," she choked out. "I'm down here!"

"I see her!" someone else shouted. "Jesus, someone get this hole open and call a chopper for evac!"

"Thank you, thank you, thank you."

Without warning, rock fell around her, chips bouncing off what used to be a cheerful blue burka. After so long, it was a muddy brown and reeked to high heaven.

"Ma'am, I'm coming down to help you. Just stay still for me, okay?"

"Bring something to cut chain," she called, sitting down to conserve her strength. She wanted to meet her rescue on her feet, but her heart pounded and she felt as if she might faint. "I'm chained to the wall."

Something struck the ground a few feet away. The end of a rope twitched, making her hope they didn't expect her to climb it. Even healthy and fit, she'd have been hard pressed to shimmy her ass up a rope.

To her surprise, a man wedged his body into the hole over her head and slid down like he did it every day. Crouching next to her, he touched her shoulder.

"Ma'am, can you tell me your name?"

She turned to look at him but saw nothing but a shaggy beard concealed by a helmet. "I'm—"

"Holy shit. You're Zinnia Turner." Jumping to his feet, he shouted, "Where's that chopper?"

"Fifteen out!"

He said another swear under his breath, then knelt and tried to help her sit up. "I'll get this chain off you in a second. Can you stand?"

"Maybe," she said dreamily, leaning against his chest. He smelled like cordite and camouflage paint, but there was a sweet, almost floral scent under the perfume of war. Like jasmine and white ginger. It was the fragrance of safety, and she relaxed, letting him take care of her. She wondered if she was hallucinating though. The scent of flowers didn't belong in a war zone.

"Send down more rope!" he shouted, tugging a pair of bolt cutters from a loop on his belt.

"You smell good." She tried to drag herself closer, but he eased her back to the ground and cut the chain. He replaced the tool in his belt, then bent to retrieve the rope his comrades dropped behind him.

"Zinnia," he said, his voice softening. "I'm going to tie this around you so I can get you out of here. Are you okay with that?"

"Your voice sounds like chocolate, and you smell like incense." She was so lightheaded with relief and the sudden absence of fear that she must have sounded like an idiot but couldn't bring herself to care.

"I'll take that as a yes," he muttered.

Carefully, he tied the ropes around her, knotting them at various points until he had her trussed into a harness. Lifting her carefully, he held her to his chest and snapped a metal clip on the rope hanging overhead.

"We've got a belay in place whenever you're ready, sir!"

"Go!"

The rope jerked, making Zinnia whimper and press her cheek against his shoulder.

"Hold on as tight as you can," he murmured into her hair.

"Do I get to go home?"

"I will take you home myself, and I promise I won't leave your side."

"Blessed be. Thank the Goddess," she whispered. Lowering her head to his chest, she let him carry her to the sky.

# CHAPTER 2

*TWO YEARS LATER...*

Sandra, her therapist, gave Zinnia a soft smile and folded her hands on her desk. "Has the aromatherapy been helping?"

"Some." Zinnia twisted a tissue in her fingers. "It's like I'm setting up for a military campaign every time I go to bed though. Nightlight, diffuser, white noise machine. Is that even normal?"

"Hey, don't knock the white noise machine. I use one." Sandra sobered, her piercing brown eyes meeting Zinnia's. "And normal is very subjective. You're still recovering from a tremendous ordeal."

"I know, but I just keep wondering when I'm going to be okay, you know?"

"Okay is just as subjective as normal, Zinnia. Two years ago, would you have thought you'd be sleeping through the night, even if it's just a few times a week?"

Zinnia nodded, acknowledging the point. "I used to love St. Louis, but it's too loud with too many people. There's almost no green space, and..." She let out a sigh and rubbed her eyes. "It shouldn't and I don't know why it does, but it reminds me of that damned cave."

"There is a lot of concrete," Sandra murmured. "Have you thought about moving somewhere out of town? Maybe across the river to Illinois or south of the city?"

"Sometimes, but my mother would throw a hissy fit. You know how she is." And it wouldn't solve Zinnia's most pressing problems because she'd still be driving into the city to work.

"She loves you. I mean, you basically came back from the dead. Do you think her desire to keep you close is out of line?"

"I guess not."

Aside from several weeks of military debriefing,

she'd had to endure multiple doctor visits, a dentist to fix her teeth, and countless meetings with accountants, attorneys, and an alphabet soup of government agencies to get her life back. Those things were exhausting, but necessary. Then there was all the professional development she needed to get her career on track. Thankfully, the clinic where she'd found work was paying her a decent wage. Her sisters had helped immeasurably too. Hyacinth let her have a studio apartment in one of her St. Charles buildings at half the usual rent, and Azalea had helped her buy a car.

It was ferociously expensive and more than a little inconvenient to come back from the dead. Her parents still tried to help financially as well, but she was determined to stand on her own two feet.

Zinnia glanced at her watch, knowing she was going to be late for lunch with her sisters. Sandra was helping though, and she never missed an appointment if she could help it. After two years of therapy, she could sometimes sleep through the night without nightmares, and her panic attacks had lessened to the point she could function. She'd even managed to almost finish her continuing ed and licensure to practice midwifery again.

"Maybe I'm just expecting everything to be like it was, and I know that isn't realistic." She gave

Sandra a weak smile. "I mean, life stopped for me three years ago, but it didn't stop for everyone else, right?"

"Your life didn't stop. It just got sidetracked for a time." Sandra pushed her glasses up her nose. "Maybe you should ask yourself a question."

"What's that?"

"Where do you want your life to take you?"

She thought about her therapist's question all the way to the restaurant, but didn't have an answer.

After giving Azalea and Hyacinth her apologies for being late, Zinnia took a sip from her glass of iced tea, wishing she could enjoy it. When did sweet tea get so damned... sweet?

It was about enough to make her gag.

"How's work going?" her sister Azalea asked, bouncing her son on her knee.

Zinnia had missed his birth because... reasons. Like almost a year being confined in a cave barely twenty miles from Kabul.

"It's fine." Zinnia picked at the bacon cheese-burger she no longer wanted. Along with a handful of dietary supplements big enough to choke a Grant's Farm Clydesdale horse, she was supposed to be eating red meat, leafy greens, and at least two oranges every day to combat her lingering anemia and vitamin deficiencies, but nothing ever sounded good.

"And any dates? Maybe a hot doctor at the clinic?"

"Zae!" Hyacinth glared at her and drew a finger across her throat in an attempt to shut her up.

"What? It's a valid question."

Zinnia loved her sisters, but sometimes they were just too much. Pulling out her phone as if she'd just received a text, she said, "Sorry to cut this short, but I need to get back to the clinic."

"Oh, come on," Azalea complained, rolling her eyes. "This happens every time we have lunch!"

"I know, and I'm sorry." Zinnia smiled at her nephew and tickled his chin. "But you know babies. They sometimes have the worst timing. Besides, I need to get the hours in for my certification, so I can—"

"We know," Hyacinth smiled and gave Zinnia's arm a loving squeeze. "So you can work on your own without a spotter."

That was almost a tiny fib. Zinnia still needed some hours, but she was within a month or two of meeting the necessary requirements, and Sandra had already cleared her to work. It was the only excuse her sisters would accept though.

"It's not like that girl hasn't delivered hundreds of babies before— Ouch!" Azalea rubbed her leg and glared at Hyacinth.

"She has to finish her continuing ed so she can keep on doing it, Zae. Quit fussing," Hyacinth said.

"Sorry, you're right." Azalea cut a chicken nugget into pieces for her son. "Will you be able to come to dinner with Dad and his new wife?"

"I'll make every effort." She grabbed her purse, then gave her sisters a wave and what she hoped was a cheerful smile. "See you soon!"

Not too soon though. And she had no intention of spending yet another uncomfortable meal with her father and his baby mama, finding a date, or making yet another failed attempt to slip herself back into her demanding extended family. Finding out her parents had split up while she'd been gone... That was too much, and she was in no hurry to talk to either of them. Maybe it was childish, but she was okay with that. All she wanted was time to put her life back together.

And maybe a little more time to forget the man who had promised not to leave her. She hadn't even learned his name, nor did she have any idea what he looked like, aside from his thick brown beard. All she remembered was his scent of jasmine incense and the feel of his strong arms carrying her into late afternoon daylight.

She was sure there was a reason he hadn't kept his promise. Maybe he went home, or the Army needed him somewhere else. It still hurt though.

Zinnia let out a breath and drove back to the clinic. She had twenty minutes before her shift started, but it never hurt to get ahead on paperwork. Goddess knew there was enough of that to go around.

It was almost a relief to settle into the small office she shared with Linda, the other nurse midwife. Filling out charts was comforting. It meant she didn't have to think until her next appointment showed up. With almost everyone still at lunch, it was quiet too.

She'd forgotten how loud St. Louis could be, and sometimes missed the silence.

Someone tapped on her door, making her jump with surprise. "Come in," she said, trying to erase her scowl. There was no point in infecting everyone else with her sour mood.

"I'm glad you're here early," the receptionist said. "We have a walk-in complaining of spotting and cramps."

"Has she been seen here before?"

"She said her regular obstetrician is out of town. She's thirty-four weeks and has insurance coverage."

"All right. Put her in room three and I'll be there in a second."

After closing her charts, Zinnia grabbed her stethoscope and tablet and strode to the exam room. She knocked softly, then opened the door and froze.

Sitting on the exam table was her... stepmother —a woman barely five years older than she was and pregnant with her half-sibling. Zinnia very nearly walked out, but her professionalism took over. She might not want her father's wife as a patient, yet she couldn't turn her back if there was something wrong. After shutting the door softly behind her, she sat on the stool facing the table.

"Hello, Allison. When did you start experiencing the cramping and spotting?" Zinnia asked, pulling up the patient information on her tablet.

"I'm actually fine. You're not answering your phone, so this seemed to be the only way to talk to you." Allison shrugged and gave her a weak smile. "Your father wants to see you. We wanted to ask if you'd consent to delivering our baby."

"I'll see him when I have time." Zinnia stood and opened the door. "As for delivering your child, I'm afraid the answer is no. It would be a conflict of interest. If you'll excuse me, the receptionist will show you out."

"Zinnia, wait!"

Tears burned behind her eyes as she shut the door in Allison's face and hurried back to her office. She couldn't decide if she was crying from anger or from hurt. Maybe it was simple frustration because nobody seemed at all interested in leaving her the hell alone. Aside from that, she was flat tired of giving people excuses.

From now on, they'd have to start taking *no* and *I don't want to* as answers.

Sitting down, she resisted the urge to throw the tablet out the window and tried to fix her emotions into something that wasn't homicidal rage. As she was practicing her deep breathing exercises, her email pinged with a message from the job search board she'd used to find her current position.

"Funny, I thought I unsubscribed from that."

She stopped scrolling for the link to remove her email from the list and stared at a job offer located in Montgomery, Vermont. Changing tabs, she looked it up on a map and winced. "Goddess, that's two hours from Montreal!"

It was also a relatively short flight from St. Louis. Close enough to come home if she needed to, and far enough away to get her interfering family off her back. Aside from that, it offered a generous relocation package, plus a furnished house.

She scanned the satellite image, smiling at the rural location. It might be way too close to the Arctic Circle for a city girl, but it looked quiet and very peaceful. Maybe it would be just what she needed.

Maybe it was where she wanted her life to go.

After a quick glance at the clock, she tapped the contact number into her phone and hit the call icon.

"Hello, this is Dr. Barber speaking."

His voice was deep, warm, and so comforting, it was almost like a hug. Pulling herself together, she said, "Hi. My name is Zinnia Turner, and I'm calling about the nurse midwife position you advertised. I'd like to set up an interview."

Of all the places Mitch could have chosen for his post-retirement vacation, Tennyson's guest cottage fifty yards away from a stocked fishing pond, a cold beer, and two of his three closest friends couldn't be beat.

He couldn't forget his daily companion either.

Her muzzle wrinkling into a doggy grin, Princess barked at him from the bank, as if asking him to come swim with her.

"Not today, Princess." Lifting his beer bottle, he tipped it toward her. "I'm having lunch with your daddy and Chelsea when they get home, then I'm getting evicted. You'll have a lady friend to play with from now on."

After almost three months of searching, Tennyson had finally managed to hire a nurse midwife. Just in time too. Chelsea was due to deliver twins later in the summer, and Kaden's wife Jennifer wasn't far behind.

As if his thoughts summoned Chelsea and Tennyson, the sound of tires on gravel heralded their return. Princess howled, then took off toward the main house to greet them. Chuckling, he followed her.

He opened the passenger door of the large SUV and helped Chelsea out. "Hey, Mama. How did things go?"

"I'm okay. What would you like for lunch?"

Mitch frowned. Chelsea looked exhausted and had dark circles under her eyes. He also didn't miss how she hung onto the vehicle as if she was about to fall. He didn't like getting into her business, but she hadn't looked well the entire time he'd been there.

"That's another five spanks, Chelsea. You know better than to tell a fib," Tennyson said as he hurried to her side. "Those spanks are adding up, and you're going to be a very sorry little girl sooner or later."

"Maybe, but you can't spank me until after I push the aliens out."

"Is there anything I can do?" Mitch asked.

"I'm putting Chelsea on bed rest for a few weeks. It's nothing serious, but she isn't resting well, and the crazy woman is out in her workshop every time I turn my back on her."

"You try sleeping with twenty pounds of kicking babies sitting on your bladder."

Tennyson swatted her backside, the gentle spank barely audible. "Behave yourself while I get you tucked in. I'll make you lunch in a few minutes."

"I can do it," Mitch offered.

"Actually, I have a favor to ask. The midwife is supposed to arrive soon. Do you mind sticking around to help her get settled before you head out to Kaden's?" He glared at Chelsea, then his face softened. "I have a naughty little girl to watch so she doesn't get into trouble."

"It's no problem at all," Mitch replied, giving

them a smile. "But don't be surprised if I come back to catch all the fish out of your pond and drink your beer."

"You're always welcome here," Chelsea said, laying a hand on her back. "It's just, well… we really need the midwife."

"The whole county does," Tennyson muttered. "I can do standard prenatal care and exams, but St. Albans is a long way to go for a birth."

"I'm happy to give up the guest house for such a noble cause. I'd only intended to stick around for another week or so anyway. It's time for me to get off my ass and become gainfully employed."

"Are you going to take Ryan up on his offer?" Chelsea asked. "He's been wanting to hire someone for weeks and he says you're a good fit for the position."

"We'll see. I'm not sure I want to live in New York. Anyway, you get settled and I'll make lunch for both of you." He walked to the door to open it for them.

"I hope Zinnia likes her birthday cake," Chelsea said. "Also, can we have pizza from Luigi's tonight? With extra anchovies? I thought we'd have a party to welcome her to Montgomery."

The knob slipped from his fingers and he spun, nearly tripping over Princess. "What did you say?"

"I asked Tennyson if we could get Luigi's to welcome—"

"No! The name! Tell me the name again."

Chelsea frowned and gave him a strange look. "Zinnia. I think her last name is Turner."

"Yes," Tennyson replied, "Zinnia Turner. She's driving from St. Louis. She served with Doctors Without Borders in Nepal and Afghanistan, and we're very fortunate she agreed to come here. She's already applied for licensure in Vermont, but—"

"Holy shit." He leaned against the door and slid to his ass on the brick stoop. Turner was a common enough last name, but combined with Zinnia... It had to be the same woman—especially given her occupation.

He remembered the feel of her frail body against his and how much he'd wanted protect and care for her. He remembered her whispered thanks in his ear as he loaded her into the chopper for the ride home.

Mostly, he remembered his promise to not leave her—a promise he hadn't been able to fulfill.

"Hey, are you okay?" Tennyson asked. "You look like you've seen a ghost."

"I have." He pushed Princess off his lap, then got

to his feet. "Zinnia Turner is the woman I pulled out of a cave the day before I left Afghanistan."

"You're kidding, right?" Tennyson shook his head. "Of all the people I could have hired. What are the odds?"

"You had to know when you looked at her work history," Mitch retorted. "Why didn't you tell me?"

"You never told me her name, and she didn't say a word about it. How was I to have known?"

"You're right. Sorry." Mitch pinched the skin between his brows and tried to get his scattered thoughts into order. "It's just... wow. We need to call Kaden. He spent almost as long looking for her as I did."

"He's going to sh..." Chelsea glanced at Tennyson, then added, "...shoot a brick."

"Good save there, baby girl." Tennyson put an arm around her waist and helped her into the house. "You're going to rest and let Mitch take care of it."

"But—"

"Do you want a party tonight or do you want to have supper in bed?" His face stern, Tennyson helped her sit in the recliner, then pulled the handle to extend the footrest. "And you won't be getting pizza or cake."

"Mean," Chelsea muttered under her breath. "Someone needs to pick up the pizzas."

"Kaden or Mitch will take care of it," Tennyson replied, tucking a blanket around her.

Mitch backed into their newly remodeled kitchen. "I'll make sandwiches."

It wasn't that he didn't want to be around while Tennyson took care of Chelsea. He just needed a minute. After texting Kaden, he gathered the sandwich ingredients and got to work, nearly cutting his thumb off when he trimmed the crusts from Chelsea's peanut butter and jelly.

Chances were good that Zinnia wouldn't recognize him. He'd shaved off his beard and gotten a haircut barely a day after he'd gotten stateside, and she'd only ever seen him in a helmet. He had to tell her though.

Most importantly, he needed to apologize for not keeping his promise.

# CHAPTER 3

*Z*innia hadn't exactly planned to take the scenic route to Montgomery, yet the minute she turned north on I-81 in Syracuse, there was nothing *but* scenic route. She wasn't complaining though.

For a woman who had spent the better portion of her adult life working in all corners of the world, she'd never been north of Cincinnati. Upstate New York was like driving into the past when America was covered with forest. Even the air smelled different—fresher somehow, and rich with life and growing things. She could see herself being happy here.

With every mile, it seemed as if the universe applauded her choice. By the time she turned east on

118 heading into Vermont, she'd seen several deer, two moose, and even a black bear with a pair of roly-poly cubs. It was as if they'd stopped at the side of the road to welcome her.

She'd gotten to dip her toes into two of the Great Lakes. The third would come when she reached Lake Champlain. Best of all, she'd been hungry—of all the crazy things. When she stopped for the night in Buffalo, a few hours past the halfway point, she devoured every bit of an oversized serving of carne asada, spicy street corn, and tortillas from a little cantina next to her motel. She'd even allowed herself a margarita. Her doctor *had* told her to up her citrus intake, after all.

In fact, the only downside to her whole trip was the nearly constant clamor of incoming text messages from her well-meaning, but incredibly irritating family. She tried to be charitable and think they were birthday wishes, but they were most likely another round of, "Zinnia is crazy."

She muted them as they came and didn't look at them or respond. Zinnia had made a promise to herself to embrace the words *no* and *I don't want to.* Even to her family.

For the first time in three years, she had a real, honest-to-Goddess cheek stretching grin on her face. It was the longest day of the year—the summer solstice—and she couldn't think of a better way to celebrate than a road trip to her new future on such a beautiful day.

So what if the snowfall up here was measured in feet? That's what four-wheel drive was for, right? It would give her an excuse to invest in some cute boots and cashmere sweaters. Maybe she'd go full-on native and buy a plaid flannel shirt and a snowmobile.

Laughing at herself, she belted out "The Lumber-jack Song," silently giving Monty Python an apology for her inability to carry a tune.

She had on oversized Audrey Hepburn sunglasses, her favorite orange maxi dress, and fabulous sandals with four-inch heels. Her hair looked amazing, and she'd been plucked, waxed, and primped until she glowed. Aside from wanting to make a good impression on Dr. Barber, she hoped that one day, the inside of her would be just as glorious as the outside.

Mama always complained that heels made Zinnia too tall—as if wearing flats would magically make her five-four instead of six-one—yet she'd worn ballet flats for the entire time she'd been in St. Louis.

*Line your lips and keep them shut. A lady doesn't draw attention. Laughing gives you wrinkles. Crying makes you look needy. Don't, don't, don't...*

Her entire family was pissed, but she'd had to get away. She'd been going nuts under the weight of their expectations. This was a place where she could just... be. She could wear heels and a dress the color of the sun that bared her arms and showed cleavage. She could wear crimson lipstick.

Slowing, she pulled into a tiny gas station with a real live signal bell next to the pump. She hadn't even recognized what the cable across the pavement was until she heard the chime. A young man, thin and gangly under a red polo shirt and tan trousers, rushed to her window.

"Check your tires and oil, ma'am?"

"Blessed be, do they do full-service gas up here?"

"Yes, ma'am." He grinned, revealing a mouthful of orthodonture. "This ain't a big city like Fort Jackson. You want your washer fluid topped off?"

"Please. And a restroom if you have one."

To her shock, he opened her door and held out a hand to help her. "Just inside and to the right. There's fresh coffee if you want some and help yourself to the cookie jar. My mom made oatmeal raisin this morning."

Still trying to wrap her head around the alternate reality she'd found, she stumbled into the tiny gas station wondering what to expect. It was too small to be a convenience store like she was used to.

This little corner of vintage Americana was more like someone's living room with comfortable chairs and an old-fashioned console television. It also had a cooler full of fishing bait, plus signage denoting it as a hunter's game check-in location.

No one in their right mind would pass by the old-fashioned pop machine that dispensed glass bottles for a dollar. There wasn't even a coin slot—it was a Mason jar without a lid and the locking mechanism on the machine had been disabled. After slipping a bill into the jar, she reached in and grabbed one, then popped the top with the opener mounted on the front of the cooler. She drank the icy cola straight from the bottle, and carefully put her empty in a crate on the floor with several others.

Incongruously, vintage Motown emanated softly from a Bluetooth speaker set on the counter. Next to it was an antique bronze cash register with a hand crank. There wasn't even a credit card reader. Instead, there was what must have been a truly ancient imprinter with paper slips.

She went into the scrupulously clean bathroom

and did her business, then grabbed a cookie from a jar shaped like a sleeping cat. Past Zinnia wouldn't have considered taking a homemade cookie from someone she didn't know, but present Zinnia…

After taking a bite of one of the best cookies she'd ever had in her mouth, she looked up and said, "I get it. You don't have to tell me twice I made the right decision."

The young man hurried in and stood behind the counter. He punched the keys, then turned the crank on the cash register. "I put a little air in your driver's side front tire. Oil is good, and I topped off your washer fluid, ma'am. That'll be $52.50, please."

Trying not to giggle at the cash register bell, she paid him, then slipped a ten-dollar bill into the tip jar. "Tell your mama she makes mighty fine cookies. Blessed be, and joyous Litha."

Grinning like her face was about to split open, Zinnia got back on the road. With luck, she could be in Montgomery in time for supper. Well, maybe she'd make it if she quit stopping at every antique store and sugar shack she found.

Finally, she made it to her new home with plenty of time to spare before she was due to meet Dr. Barber. It was about the cutest little town she'd ever seen, filled with sloping roofs and brick storefronts that looked like they hadn't changed in a hundred years. The only stop she allowed herself was a small grocery store for a few things to tide her over until she could put together a list for the Costco almost an hour away.

Zinnia would be living in Dr. Barber's guest house, but she didn't want to take advantage of his hospitality and show up for breakfast in the morning because she'd forgotten coffee and milk.

Dr. Barber lived a few miles out of town on a winding road shaded by gorgeous maples. Slowing, she looked for the mailbox he'd described. It was supposed to be wood with a statue of a forest nymph on top. Strange, but who was she to judge?

Finally, she found it, but had to stop and examine the carving. Looking at it from the road, it was sweet and whimsical. Yet as she got closer, details sprang out. Barely concealed by a wing folded over her torso, the nymph had her hand between her thighs and a great big orgasm face. The sexual elements of the carving were hidden in plain sight, but someone would have to get very close to pick them out.

She giggled and covered her mouth with her hand, then got back into her car, trying to keep a straight face. It seemed Dr. Barber had a naughty sense of humor, and she couldn't wait to meet him.

After making her way down the curving drive-way, she parked next to the main house and got a good look at the cottage that would be hers until she found a permanent residence. Standing about fifty yards from the main house, it looked like a field-stone dollhouse sitting on the banks of a charming little pond. The windows were trimmed with flowerboxes spilling over with morning glories, and the steeply pitched roof was shingled with slate tiles.

The main house was almost exactly the same construction but was about twice the size and had an expansive deck facing the pond. As she got out of her vehicle, a large husky with blue eyes and a wagging tail bounded out to meet her. Crouching, she scratched the dog's ears, noting in passing that it was female.

"Well, aren't you a pretty princess?"

"Welcome to Vermont. Looks like you've made a friend, and you even guessed her name."

Smiling, Zinnia stood and brushed off her hands. The man was a few inches shorter than she was, with spiky black hair laced with a few threads of gray at the temples and a round face. Muscles bulged under his T-shirt, communicating strength in his sexily compact body.

The libido she'd thought dead and gone perked up, and she firmly reminded herself that this person was both her boss, and happily married. Yet there was something about him that seemed strangely familiar, even though she'd have sworn she'd never met him.

"Hi, Dr. Barber? I'm Zinnia Turner."

"No. I'm Mitch Sakurai, Tennyson's friend. He asked me to help you get settled, and I was hoping to get a chance to talk to you."

He held out his hand and she took it.

She'd always thought that romantic cliché about sparks flying when someone touched their one true love was silly, but a thousand volts coursed up her arm when he shook her hand. An errant breeze blew his scent toward her, and she inhaled sharply, suddenly thrust back to a filthy cave in Afghanistan.

Her heart stalled in her chest and instead of jasmine, she smelled the dusty stone of her cave. The sunlight seemed to vanish, and she staggered, feeling links of chain around her ankle.

She heard a keening whine and tried to focus on where her logical brain told her she was. Vermont.

She was in Vermont, and it was Litha—not Ostara—and the whine was coming from her.

"Orange dress, high heels," she whispered, praying that was what she'd see when she looked down at herself instead of a muddy brown burka that used to be blue.

And she prayed for the man who smelled like jasmine incense.

ZINNIA STUMBLED on her skyscraper heels, nearly falling into him.

"Whoa! Are you okay?"

"J-jasmine incense," she whispered, a single tear sliding down her cheek. She wiped it away with a finger and stared at it as if the wetness surprised her. "I remember you. You saved my life, and then you vanished."

Mitch winced, then offered her his arm. He'd meditated for years with the jasmine incense that reminded him of his grandfather's house in Kyoto and didn't really notice the scent anymore, but she'd obviously remembered. "Let's go inside and we'll talk. You look like you could use a cup of tea, and maybe an explanation."

Thankfully, she seemed to snap out of her shock and laid a hand on his arm, letting him help her to the guest house. When they reached it, he held the door, allowing her to go first.

Her sandals were gorgeous, but they weren't going to be much use on Tennyson's gravel drive-way. Worse, she might hurt her pretty red-painted toes.

She was inappropriately dressed for rural Vermont, but fantastically so. Elegant, and so damned gorgeous it threatened to stop his heart, she wouldn't have been out of place on a catwalk at a fashion show.

Her heels clicked on the maple flooring as she approached the couch. Seating herself, she said, "Maybe I could have a tiny glass of bourbon instead of tea?"

"The closest I have is beer, I'm afraid. Want one?"

"Please."

Hurrying to the kitchen, he grabbed two bottles from the fridge and opened them. After handing her one, he sat across from her in an armchair.

"You look—"

"How have you—"

Her eyes crinkled with amusement and she tilted her bottle toward him. "You first."

"I was about to say you look amazing. It's wonderful to see you so healthy and happy."

"Thank you." She took a sip from her beer. "How have you been?"

"Good. I'm retired now. I came up here for a short vacation before I do something more productive with my time and get a job."

"What do you do?"

"Computers. Mostly tech support and server maintenance, but I wrote specialized apps for the military. Nothing fancy like delivering babies."

She looked away, then gave him a brilliant and very false smile. "Anyway, you and Dr. Barber are friends?"

"We've known each other for about ten years. A mutual friend introduced us at—" He cut himself off before he told her about Saints and Sinners, the bondage club where he'd met Ryan, Tennyson, and Kaden, then said, "We were introduced in New York."

"I didn't go that way. I turned almost straight north in Syracuse. It was very tempting to go to Canada just to say I'd been there, but there was a line at the border crossing."

"You should have stopped to see Niagara Falls

when you were in Buffalo. Tennyson would have understood."

"Oh, I did, but from the American side. I wasn't about to pass that up."

"Good." Mitch fell silent, unsure what to say to the woman he'd thought about for going on three years, yet who was also a complete stranger.

After setting her beer on a coaster, she stood and looked around. "This is a really cute little house," she murmured.

"Want a tour?"

"Um, sure?"

"The kitchen is right through that door," he replied, thankful for the out. "The laundry is in the mudroom, and there's a root cellar. It's a mess, but that's where the water shutoff and the boiler are. The bedrooms and bathroom are this way."

"Would anyone mind if I played this?" she asked, running a long-fingered hand over the yellowed ivory keys of the antique spinet piano in the living room.

"I doubt it. It belonged to Tennyson's great-grandmother, Edith. They moved it here to keep it out of the construction mess when they remodeled their kitchen, but I don't think either of them play."

She paused and played a sweeping arpeggio, then smiled. "It's gorgeous. Thank you."

"No problem." He led her down the hall and pointed the rooms out. Her eyes lit up at the claw-foot tub in the single bathroom.

"I appreciate the tour. I guess I better unpack my car and get settled in. You probably want to get on with your day."

Laying a hand on her arm, he stopped her before she could walk outside. "There's something else. Can we sit?"

"Okay." She arched a brow and gave him a questioning glance but followed him.

Instead of sitting across from her, he joined her on the couch. He drew in a breath, then let it out. "I apologize for not keeping my promise, Zinnia. I couldn't get back to the base fast enough to catch you before they sent you home, and then I was ordered not to contact you."

She was silent for several seconds and looked at her hands. Zinnia was so still, and he almost reached for her, but he wasn't sure if he'd send her into another panic attack. Finally, she straightened and looked up, then nodded. "I understand. Just one of those things, right?"

"No, I made you a promise, Zinnia. I should have kept it, and for that, I owe you an apology."

To his horror, she burst into tears, curling up with her knees against her chest. Her sobs broke his heart, and without considering whether his actions would be welcomed, he pulled her into his lap. Turning in his arms, she lowered her head to his shoulder. Her tears dampened his shirt, but he ignored it.

"Shh, baby girl, it's going to be okay." Aside from that, he simply rocked her and let her cry. It was the only thing he could think to do that might have been helpful.

Eventually, she sat up and wiped her eyes with the back of her hand, then eased herself from his lap and sat next to him. She sniffed and gave him a watery smile, then said, "I promise, I'm not usually crazy. I don't make a habit of sobbing on the shoulders of almost perfect strangers."

He wanted to pull her back into his lap, but aside from barely knowing her, she needed space. "You're not crazy. I—"

A knock interrupted him a split second before the door burst open. His hair disheveled, Kaden fixed his eyes on Zinnia and strode across the room, then pulled her to her feet and swept her into a tight hug.

"Zinnia! Fuck! I can't believe you're here!" He put his hands on her head and kissed her cheeks, then hugged her again. "Welcome home, baby girl. You have no idea—"

Jerking out of Kaden's arms, Zinnia backed away. "Mitch, who is this person?"

She looked terrified, and he jumped to his feet to get between her and Kaden to make sure she had a little space, furious that Kaden had frightened her. "This is Kaden McCleod. He spent some time looking for you too."

Zinnia's lip quivered as she stepped into Mitch's arms. "I'm... sorry, you surprised me."

"Ignore him," Jennifer said, walking in. "I'm sorry he tackle hugged you. I'm the big lug's wife, Jennifer, and I promise he won't do it again. If he does, I'll give all his fancy shoes to the new litter of puppies in the clinic."

"And I'll spank your butt, little girl. You don't touch a man's shoes."

Ignoring him, Jennifer held up a bottle of wine. "I can't have any, but I come bearing alcohol. Want some liquid courage to make up for my husband scaring the life from you? You might need it for Chelsea's welcome party too."

Mitch kept his arms around her, feeling her shudder as he considered whether or not he should kick Kaden's ass for scaring her. "You okay, honey?"

"Yeah." She eased herself from his arms. "I'm just not great with surprises."

As if realizing how much he'd frightened Zinnia, Kaden flushed. "I... um, I'm sorry. I'm just delighted to finally meet you."

She blinked and a tremulous smile blossomed on her lips. "It's okay. What's this I hear about a welcome party?"

"Chelsea is planning it, but you need wine first," Jennifer said. "If you drink enough, I can convince you to take a puppy to go with your new house. Or maybe a kitten if that's more your speed. I also have a miniature horse that could use a new home, and—"

Kaden gave Jennifer a mock scowl and swatted her butt. "I can't take you anywhere. Behave yourself, little girl, and stop trying to give people pets."

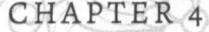

## CHAPTER 4

*M*ore tears burned behind Zinnia's eyes, but these were happy tears. She was still overwhelmed and off balance, but Kaden and Jennifer were so incredibly refreshing.

They didn't ask how she was feeling or look at her like she might explode into a fit of rage, or try to talk her down before she did something embarrassing in public. Her cousin Trevor even asked her if she was off her meds once—as if he fully expected her be happy and laughing after what had happened to her.

She'd always suspected Trevor's mama had dropped him on his head a time or three.

Kaden even apologized for the unexpected physical contact—something her family never did when they surprised her—and went right back to paying attention to his wife as if he hadn't almost made her fight or flight instincts kick in. It happened, he moved on, and didn't treat her any differently than someone he might have talked to on the street.

Blessed be, she needed that. And she'd needed Mitch. The way he put himself between her and his friend was swoon-worthy, not to mention how he'd held her when she broke down. It was embarrassing, yet she hadn't realized how much she needed someone to just hold her and make her feel safe.

"Come on," Jennifer said, "let's go sit in the kitchen so I can ply you with wine. You can tell me where you got that fabulous dress."

"Since when did you ever wear dresses?" Kaden shot back, grinning at her.

"Since you foisted this baby bump on me, and my work coveralls don't fit. Even my scrubs are tight," Jennifer retorted.

"They make maternity scrubs. I can hook you up," Zinnia replied, charmed by the tiny woman. "Do you work in the medical field?"

"I'm a veterinarian. My patients are a bit more likely to bite than humans, but only somewhat."

Laughing, Zinnia followed her into the kitchen

and found a corkscrew in a drawer. "I've never had a pet, but I love animals."

There was no way her parents would have allowed an animal into the house, but Zinnia had still put a puppy or kitten on her Christmas list every year when she was a kid.

Jennifer blinked as if she couldn't understand the statement. "Are you allergic?" she finally asked.

"No, my parents just never wanted animals in the house, and once I was on my own, I joined Doctors Without Borders."

"Hmm." Jennifer found a wineglass and filled it, then passed it over. "If you're not ready for a pet, you could volunteer. I run a small shelter attached to my clinic, and we always need people to help out."

"I might take you up on the offer once I get settled in."

"There's no rush." She smiled and gave Zinnia's wineglass a longing glance. "Anyway, I want to apologize again for Kaden. Not finding you was one of his regrets, but he shouldn't have touched you like that."

"No, it's okay. I just…" Zinnia let her voice trail off, unsure of what she wanted to say. "It just surprised me."

"He's lucky you didn't punch his lights out."

Snorting, Zinnia took a sip of wine. "I almost did."

"He'd have had it coming. Anyway, where did you get that dress? I love that color on you."

After handing Jennifer her phone, Zinnia said, "Give me your number and I'll text you the link."

"Thanks!" Jennifer typed her number in, then said, "Finish up your wine. Chelsea talked Tennyson into pizza from Luigi's and unless you're dying, you don't want to miss it."

"Luigi's?"

"It's the best Chicago pie you'll ever eat. Hopefully, she remembered to get the anchovies on the side this time. Although..." Jennifer licked her lips, then wrinkled her nose. "Why the hell do they sound good? I hate anchovies."

"You're pregnant. About twenty weeks, I'm thinking, but I'd need your date of conception to be sure."

"Good guess! That's what Tennyson said, but that whole pregnancy craving thing is bullshit."

"Your body probably wants the salt and calcium."

"But anchovies? That's so weird."

"I assure you; it isn't. Eat whatever sounds good, as long as it's actually food and isn't on the list of things pregnant women should avoid. If you find yourself wanting to eat something that isn't normally edible, we'll talk."

"Ew. Does that ever happen?"

"I've had expectant mothers craving chalk before, so yes, it's possible."

"You will definitely be the first to know. Thankfully, none of my favorites are on the no-no list." Jennifer gave her a wicked grin, then added, "I'm going to eat the anchovies and let Kaden suffer my fishy breath for the evening. He deserves it."

Zinnia chuckled and finished her wine. "Fish breath it is. I'm going to get my stuff from my car and change my shoes. I think I'm overdressed."

"Looks like Kaden and Mitch already took care of it," Jennifer replied, pointing out the kitchen window at the two men carrying her things into the cottage. "Hope you brought a swimsuit. We'll probably take a dip in the pond later. Tennyson has a rope swing set up, but Kaden won't let me use it anymore because of the baby."

The remark made Zinnia remember the spank Kaden had given Jennifer and she frowned. She'd been too overwhelmed to register it at first. Hopefully, it was her imagination, but she was bound by law to report suspected abuse.

"Well, hopefully, he won't spank you again."

Jennifer smirked, then got up for a glass of water. "It's a common occurrence. He's really overprotective, and my job isn't exactly risk-free."

Reaching over the table, she touched Jennifer's hand. "Hey, have a question for you. Is there something you want to tell me while Kaden isn't around?"

"No, we pretty much tell each other everything. Why?"

"Do you need a safe place to go? I can—"

"Oh, my God. You think he's abusive." She squeezed Zinnia's hand and shook her head violently. "No. Just hell to the no. I realize Kaden is imposing and overbearing. He's definitely in trouble for touching you the way he did, but he would never harm a woman or child. I know that better than I know my own name."

"Well… okay. I'm sorry if I offended you, but when I saw him spank you…" Zinnia shrugged, then added, "I had to ask."

"Don't knock it until you try it," Jennifer muttered under her breath.

Zinnia didn't think she'd been meant to hear that, but she had to make sure Jennifer was safe. "You don't have to agree to being spanked, Jennifer. If he's hurting you—"

"The first time he spanked me was because of Chelsea," Jennifer interrupted. "Her ex shot Princess, and Chelsea brought her to my clinic on Christmas eve. When I finished the surgery, I was so damned mad…" Her hands tightened into fists and her face darkened. "It might have been Chelsea instead of her dog."

She touched Zinnia's hand and met her eyes, her expression earnest. "I was so pissed, I went outside during a blizzard in nothing but Crocs and scrubs to chop wood. Kaden stopped me, and he spanked my butt when I argued. Then he held me on his lap while I cried it out."

"I see." Hopefully, Zinnia had been wrong. It seemed as if their relationship was consensual, in which case, it was none of her business. "But he did spank you until you cried."

"I didn't cry because he spanked me, and truthfully, it didn't really hurt. I cried because I was terrified and furious for Chelsea." Jennifer stood and put the wine bottle in the fridge.

"I don't think I understand."

"I didn't at first either." Jennifer peeked out the window to make sure Kaden and Mitch were still occupied. "He takes care of me, makes sure I eat properly, get enough sleep, and all that other bullshit

57

that comes with having a demanding full-time job. It's... I can't really explain it."

"He's not doing anything without your educated consent, right?"

"Absolutely not. Kaden is my Daddy, and I love him very much." Winking, she added, "Besides, a smart man doesn't mess with a woman who keeps veterinary sedatives and scalpels in her work truck."

Zinnia laughed, but the way Jennifer said the word *daddy* resonated with her. It was obviously a term of endearment and had meaning for them. She'd never really understood what would make a grown-ass woman agree to a Daddy dynamic, yet she wasn't one to kink-shame either.

Still, her heart raced with longing. She wanted someone so attuned to her needs that he would comfort her like that.

*Like Mitch did.*

"I'm sorry. I didn't mean to pry, but as a medical professional, I have to ask."

"Don't worry about it. I actually have to follow similar rules, but you know, with animals." She took Zinnia's glass and washed it, then put it away. "Anyway, did Mitch get all his stuff moved out?"

"What? I don't understand." She corked the bottle and put it in the fridge.

"He's been living here for the last couple of weeks. Kaden and I are putting him up in our guest room until he decides where he wants to work."

"Oh, no! I didn't mean to kick him out."

"He's just visiting anyway, so I'm sure he doesn't mind."

Maybe Jennifer was right, but Zinnia still felt like a heel.

"So," Kaden said, pulling a box from the back of Zinnia's SUV, "do I need to beat the shit out of you for making Zinnia cry?"

"How did you know?"

"Please. Her eyes were all swollen and she was sniffing."

Mitch grabbed a second box, grunting at the weight. It wasn't particularly surprising Kaden had left him the one clearly labeled as medical texts. "I messed up, but I apologized. Then she started crying."

"You mean she hasn't been here a day and you've already fucked up?"

"No, that fuck-up happened in Afghanistan. I promised her I wouldn't leave her when I put her on an evac chopper. By the time I got my men back to base, she was already on a plane to Ramstein. After that, I was ordered not to contact her."

"Hmm." Kaden followed him back to Zinnia's vehicle and helped him grab the rest of her belongings. "Sounds more like she left without you, but the Army is good for screwing up a perfectly good plan. Maybe she just got overwhelmed at seeing you again."

"Maybe." Mitch had his doubts. Even if she'd seen someone for counseling, there was no way she was completely recovered.

"At least she'll have some space now. Tennyson and Chelsea won't bother her." Kaden went silent as a dreamy smile crossed his scarred face. "That's why I came up here. Peace and quiet. Then I found everything I didn't know I wanted."

Maybe there was a way he could make his failure up to her. "Can you get the rest of Zinnia's stuff? I have to send a quick message."

"Sure, there's only a couple of suitcases left anyway."

He brought up the email from a company in St. Albans, then typed a quick reply accepting their job offer. It didn't pay as well as some of the others, but it would mean he could keep his promise to Zinnia—well, if she wanted him to. If she didn't, he'd still be close to Kaden and Tennyson.

After putting his phone away, he hurried to help Kaden with the last of her things. By the time they had everything in the house, she and Jennifer were waiting.

"Thanks," Zinnia said softly. "It wasn't necessary, but I appreciate you unloading everything."

"Suitcases in the bedroom?" Kaden asked.

"Yes, the larger one on the right, please. The windows in the smaller one face east and south. Not great if you want to sleep in," Mitch said.

Turning to him, she chewed on her lower lip for a moment, then said, "I don't want you to have to move just because of me. If you want, we can share the house. You can have the bigger room until you're ready to leave."

"It's no problem. I'm happy staying with Kaden and—"

"No, I'll feel guilty forever. Besides, I'm always up at dawn anyway." She lowered her head and clasped her hands. "I like to see the sun rise."

Of course, she did. She hadn't been able to for too long. "Are you sure? I really don't mind moving."

"No!" She slapped a hand over her mouth when

Jennifer and Kaden turned at her shout. "Please. I'm sorry, but… I don't want to be alone."

"Okay." He studied her worried face for a moment, then added, "Do you need a hug?"

"Yeah, maybe I do."

"Then come here and get one." Mitch held out his arms, hoping she'd step into them. He had no intention of taking it as Kaden had done, so she had to make the first move.

To his relief, she moved close and laid her head on his shoulder. He didn't hear Jennifer and Kaden slip away, and only noticed their absence when the door shut behind them. Zinnia's rigid spine relaxed, and she inhaled deeply.

"I'm sorry, I—"

He wrapped his arms around her, squeezing gently. To his dismay, his cock hardened the minute she pressed herself against him. Shifting his weight, he angled his hips away from her.

"Shh. Don't ever be sorry for asking for what you need. I promise, I'll do everything in my power to make sure you have it."

She laughed softly and pulled away. He let her go, despite the overwhelming urge to keep her in his arms. She needed time, space, and understanding.

"I think that's a more realistic promise," she murmured. "Thank you."

Grimacing, he nodded. "Leave it to the Army to spoil my plans. It never occurred to me they'd ship you out so fast."

"I was told there was a plane leaving and they wanted me on it. At least they let me have time for a shower and gave me clean clothes, but I wasn't about to argue."

"And you shouldn't have. I just wanted to be the one to escort you to St. Louis."

Cocking her head, she blinked. "How did you know I'm from St. Louis?"

His cheeks warmed and he gave her a shame-faced grin. "I might or might not have stalked your social media, hoping I'd find you someday."

He wasn't about to admit he'd thought she was dead. It would be hurtful and unproductive.

Zinnia laughed outright and a gorgeously wide smile made her glow. "My folks turned my Facebook into a memorial page. It was such a mess trying to get it restored that I eventually gave up. It wasn't like I used it anyway, but I wish my mother hadn't put all my childhood pictures up. That was embarrassing to find."

"I bet." Privately, he wanted to have words with

her parents for the insensitive act, yet he understood it and couldn't imagine what she'd gone through to get her life back. "We can head to the main house whenever you're ready. There's no rush."

"I just need to scare up a swimsuit and sneakers. These heels aren't going to do."

"Do you need help?"

"Nope. I'm good." She turned and walked toward the bedrooms. "You could bring your stuff back in if you're sure you don't mind staying with the crazy lady."

Without conscious thought, Mitch caught up to her, then crowded her into a corner. He pinched her chin between two fingers, forcing her to look at him. "You are not crazy," he gritted out. "You're strong and resilient, and anyone who says otherwise will have to deal with me."

"But—"

"And that includes you, baby girl."

# CHAPTER 5

Zinnia should have been insulted by the endearment. She was an adult, and being called baby girl should have had her taking Mitch down a peg.

Except coming from him, it was filled with... caring. It wasn't disrespectful. It wasn't rude, and it sure as fuck wasn't patronizing. It was sweet and simple.

It was kind.

"Can I say I have issues?" she asked, pushing the words past the lump in her throat.

He smiled, making the skin around his eyes crease. "Right now, your biggest issue is a serious lack of Luigi's pizza and a dip in the pond."

He laid a hand on the small of her back and

directed her into the larger of the two bedrooms where he and Kaden had left her belongings. "Find your swimsuit and I'll bring my stuff back in."

Reminding herself to move her luggage to the other bedroom, she fished out the closest thing she had to a swimsuit, plus a pair of white sneakers. The bright yellow sports bra and booty shorts covered more than most bikinis, and she could wear them under her dress.

She changed quickly and was tying her shoes by the time she heard Mitch's footsteps. After zipping her suitcase, she extended the handle and pulled it from the room.

"I'm just about ready," she said as he walked toward her carrying a large duffle bag. "I figured I'd move my stuff before I forget later."

"Are you sure you're good with the small room? I don't mind taking it."

"Yeah, I'd have probably picked that one anyway so I could see the sun." She left her suitcase on the floor next to a double sleigh bed covered with a patchwork quilt. The only bad thing about this room was the bed—she wasn't sure it was quite long enough for her to stretch out without her feet dangling off the edge. The queen bed in the larger room wouldn't be much better though.

He followed with her other suitcase, then held out an arm. "Ready to meet your new neighbors?"

*No.*

She pushed her nerves aside. Everyone had been more than kind, and she couldn't imagine Dr. Barber or his wife being any different. "Sure. I've been here over an hour, and I haven't met my new boss yet. I want to thank him for giving me such a wonderful place to stay."

"He's just happy someone is living in it. The last time it stood empty for any length of time, the pipes in the kitchen burst and flooded the cellar."

"Yikes! What a mess!"

"Chelsea got it straightened out. She's one of the best building contractors in northern Vermont, but most of her business is custom sculpture and art these days. People from all over the world buy her work, and she even has a few pieces featured in a resort called Club Apocalypse in Arizona."

"Oh, how fascinating. I can't wait to meet her. What does she make?"

"Did you see the nymph on the mailbox?"

She bit her lip and tried not to smile, then decided to play innocent. "Yes, it was lovely."

Mitch winked at her as if he was about to call her on her bullshit. "Well, just keep an open mind, and don't stare at her carvings for too long. They're mesmerizing like hidden object games, and you'll see something different every time you look at them."

They reached the front door of the main house as he finished speaking. Before they could knock, the door swung open to reveal Jennifer.

"Come on in! We're set up on the deck, and Kaden should be back with the pizza shortly."

"If he knows what's good for him," a blonde woman, clearly pregnant, standing behind her said. "I'm starving."

She looked to be well into her second trimester and had long, curly hair, and the prettiest green eyes Zinnia had ever seen. Waddling closer, she held out a hand. "I'm Chelsea Barber, and you must be Zinnia. It's such a pleasure to finally meet you. Would you mind telling the aliens it's time to come out so I can get back to work?"

"The aliens?" Zinnia asked, trying not to smile.

"Yeah. These two little girls playing soccer with my bladder. Speaking of which, excuse me."

"Chelsea, did I not tell you to stay in the recliner?" a man asked from the other room.

"Bathroom break, Daddy!"

Before she could think too hard about both

Chelsea and Jennifer using the same endearment for their husbands, a very tall man stepped forward and smiled. He had thick dark hair and blue eyes surrounded by laugh lines. He was also a good four inches taller than Zinnia, which was unusual enough to be noteworthy.

"Dr. Barber?" she asked. "It's good to meet you."

"Call me Tennyson." He took her hand in a massive paw and gave it a gentle shake.

The sound of his deep, comforting voice made her laugh inwardly at herself. Dr. Barber sounded just as he had during their telephone interview, and she couldn't believe she'd mistaken Mitch for him.

"Thank you. And thank you for the use of your guest cottage. It's beautiful."

"It's my pleasure. I'm just happy to have someone living there to keep an eye on it."

"Well, I'll have help. Mitch agreed to stay in the other bedroom." She swallowed, then added, "If you'll allow it, I mean."

Zinnia hid a wince when he pinned Mitch with a steady gaze. She'd probably overstepped by asking before clearing the idea with Dr. Barber. After all, it wasn't exactly her house.

To her relief, he nodded and gave her a smile. "As

long as you're okay with it, it's fine by me. Just remember, there's only one bathroom."

"I'm sure we can set up a schedule," Mitch replied, moving slowly to cup her elbow.

He made sure she could see every movement he made so he didn't touch her without warning. It wasn't that she was touch averse—she just didn't like to be surprised. Somehow, he'd recognized it and was giving her the support she needed without coming on too strong.

Until she'd been snatched off the streets in front of her hospital, she'd had an active, albeit private, sex life. She liked men and loved sex. Never in her life had she experienced such an immediate attraction for someone, and she wondered if it had been a good idea to ask him to stay with her.

There were too many things she was still afraid of. But mostly, she was afraid of being alone.

It was completely bass ackward. She'd wanted space from her family and from the overloud, overcrowded city, but the thought of being in a house by herself made her pulse race with anxiety.

"You guys go on out," Tennyson said, interrupting her reverie. "I'll bring Chelsea when she's done in the bathroom. Also, Zinnia, if you're up to it Monday morning, I'd like you to give her a thorough exam. She's demanding a home birth, but with twins…"

"I haven't gotten my licensure back from Vermont yet, but my professional development is done. As long as you act as the attending physician, and there isn't anything going on that would require a hospital, it'll be fine."

"That was fast! You must have worked yourself to the bone."

She had, but she decided not to mention it. Changing the subject, Zinnia said, "You have a lovely home. Princess was even kind enough to greet me when I parked."

He glanced at the floor and smiled. "Have you met—"

Something warm and heavy sat on her foot and she flinched. She looked down at a large and very fluffy golden retriever and let out a slightly hysterical laugh. Goddess have mercy, her nerves.

"Caleb, don't sit on the nice nurse midwife," Jennifer reached for the dog's collar, but Zinnia shook her head.

"No, it's okay." She bent down to scratch his ears. "He's sweet as candy."

Somehow, just being able to touch the dog made her heart rate slow and she could almost feel the dopamine coursing through her brain. There was a reason animals like Caleb were used in clinical applications for their beneficial effect on patients. She'd seen it hundreds of times.

It was almost as good as one of Mitch's hugs.

Straightening, she smiled at Jennifer. "I'm thinking maybe I want a pet of my own."

JENNIFER CLAPPED her hands and beamed. "Let's go outside. I'll tell you all about who we have available for adoption."

As the ladies walked through the kitchen to the French doors leading to the deck, Tennyson gave him a look. "I'm not sure how I feel about you moving in on Zinnia like that."

"I'm not moving in on her." Mitch tried not to snap at his friend, but wasn't sure he was successful at controlling the tone of his voice.

"Hmm." Tennyson folded his hands behind his back. "Just so you're aware, Kaden and I will both kick your ass if you do something to make our midwife leave."

"No, it's nothing like that." Mitched rubbed his face and watched Zinnia chatting happily with

Jennifer and Chelsea. "She asked, and I couldn't say no."

It could never be anything like what Tennyson was implying. He was too old for her, for one thing. For another, she needed space and time to pull herself together without having a near stranger paw at her.

He started forward, meaning to join the ladies, but Tennyson laid a hand on his arm. "Also, today is Zinnia's thirtieth birthday. Chelsea had Mrs. Parker bake a cake, but I'm not sure if we should bring it out. How do you think she'll react?"

How had he not remembered that? Maybe it was just the shock of seeing Zinnia in person. "Who's Mrs. Parker?"

"The wife of the owner of the hardware store where Chelsea used to work. Her cinnamon rolls are a mouthful of heaven. Anyway, what do you think?"

"I honestly have no idea. Do you have candles?"

"Probably not thirty of them, but yes. Chelsea likes them."

"Good. We'll have it after supper. Cross your fingers she takes it in the spirit it's intended."

Kaden soon arrived with four enormous pizza boxes. As if they were sharks smelling blood in the water, the ladies' heads snapped around. He squeezed his eyes shut dramatically and shuddered. "Cover me. I'm going in."

Mitch chuckled and held the door for him. "Seems like a lot of pizza for six people."

"Have you seen Jennifer and Chelsea eat recently? Anyway, I got one with double anchovies for Chelsea and three without, plus an extra order of the nasty little fishies on the side."

"I heard that!" Chelsea said.

"I'm sure you did, little girl." Smiling broadly, Kaden laid the boxes on the table. "The one on top has double anchovies, just for you, and the extras are in the bag with the parmesan knots."

"You are now forgiven, and a god among men." Chelsea opened the box and put two slices on her plate. To Mitch's surprise, Jennifer dug in as well, wolfing the food down like she'd been starving.

Zinnia laughed and took a slice from one of the anchovy-free pizzas. "Eat up, ladies. This looks delicious. Will you gentlemen be joining us?"

"We'll wait until you're finished," Tennyson said, obviously trying to hide a smile. "We'd hate to lose a hand in the feeding frenzy."

Mitch loved seeing Zinnia like that. Her shoulders dropped and she sprawled in her chair with her long legs stretched out in front of her. Caleb had his head in her lap, and she stroked his ears as she ate. The tightness around her eyes and mouth was gone, and she looked relaxed and completely at peace.

He pulled up a chair and sat next to her, then risked life and limb to grab a slice of pizza. "Having fun?" he asked softly.

She swallowed and dabbed her lips with a napkin. "I'm having a great time. You were right about Luigi's pizza too."

"There's more if you want it."

"No, thank you. I'm good." To his surprise, she leaned over and kissed his cheek. "Thank you for introducing me to your friends."

Getting his mind back on business and off the burgeoning erection in his jeans, he shook his head. "I'm just a visitor. You live here now."

"True." She grabbed a parmesan knot and swiped it through a cup of marinara. "Everyone has been so kind. The gas station attendant I met somewhere in New York even gave me homemade cookies."

"Oh?"

"It was full-service gas with an oil check and everything. Have you heard of such a thing these days?" She popped the bread into her mouth, letting out a sexy little moan of pleasure. After swallowing, she said, "It's ridiculous, but it seemed like the universe was welcoming me to New England from the minute I turned north in Syracuse."

Giving him a pointed look, Tennyson collected the pizza boxes and carried them inside. Unwilling to let her be blindsided by the surprise, Mitch leaned close to whisper, "Tennyson told me it's your birthday and he has a surprise planned. If it's going to weird you out, I'll tell him not to."

Her eyes widened and she gave him a tremulous smile. "Blessed be, I... I don't know what to say."

"Is that good or bad?"

"I have no idea." She grabbed her beer and took a long drink.

"It involves cake and birthday candles."

She snorted, then coughed to clear her throat. "How can I refuse cake and birthday candles?"

"It's easy. You just say no, and Chelsea eats your cake for breakfast."

Nodding, she tightened her fingers in Caleb's ruff, making him move his head deeper into her lap. "I'm okay but thank you for the warning."

"No problem." She leaned against him, and almost against his will, he wrapped his arm around her shoulder. "We can bail whenever you want. Just say the word and I'll take you home."

"I'm... I'm really okay." She said the words as if they surprised her.

Maybe they did.

"Someone has a special day today," Tennyson announced, coming outside with a white-frosted cake on a platter. Kaden followed with a stack of fresh plates and flatware. Three unlit birthday candles were stuck in the top, along with her name in swirly pink letters.

Tennyson set the cake in the center of the table and lit the candles. "Happy birthday, Zinnia!"

Wetness gleamed in her eyes and her red-glossed lips turned up into a smile. "Thank you. I... this is wonderful."

"Don't blow out the candles yet!" Chelsea said. "We have to sing happy birthday." She started the song, and everyone joined in.

"Make a wish, Zinnia!" Jennifer said.

Closing her eyes, Zinnia leaned forward and blew out the candles, grinning when everyone cheered. Mitch helped serve out slices and gave Zinnia the first piece.

She took a bite and closed her eyes. "Blessed be, this is good. How did y'all know lemon is my favorite?"

"Lucky guess, I suppose," Tennyson murmured. "Happy birthday, Zinnia."

"Thank you. I think this is the nicest birthday party I've ever had."

"We can even go swimming after," Chelsea said. "Well, everyone except me." She shot Tennyson a glare and stuck out her lower lip, then added, "The big meanie-head doctor won't let me."

"Actually, as long as the water is safe for swimming and isn't too cold, it can be very beneficial even during early labor. You can—"

"Yay! First dibs on the rope swing!"

"—not get on the rope swing," Zinnia finished, giving Tennyson a wink over Chelsea's head. "You can stay in for thirty minutes as long as you don't do anything strenuous, and someone will have to help you in and out to make sure you don't fall. Same goes for you, Jennifer, but you're probably okay to get in by yourself as long as someone is nearby. It will be too cold to swim by the time you need help with your balance."

"I told you so, little girl," Tennyson muttered.

Nodding, Kaden added, "We both told you so."

Mitch hid a smile at the mulish expressions on Jennifer's and Chelsea's faces. "You're no fun," Chelsea finally said.

Zinnia reached over and squeezed her shoulder. "I know, but it's better than nothing, right? And you might be able to play on the swing later in the summer."

"I'll have to wait until next year," Jennifer said, pouting. "I'm not due until October. I suppose that means no horseback riding either."

"That's a definite no," Zinnia said firmly.

"I like her," Kaden said, grinning at Tennyson. "Can we keep her?"

Laughing, Zinnia swiped a finger through the icing left on her plate and sucked it clean, then wiped her hands. "I'm going to try out that rope swing for myself. I've never done it before."

Her laughter was infectious, and he couldn't help but join in. She was just as he'd imagined her when he stalked her social media memorial page. Vivacious, charming, and so beautiful it made his chest ache.

## CHAPTER 6

"**Y**ou can change in the house if you want," Chelsea said.

Her cute little pout had vanished, but Zinnia still felt guilty for telling her she couldn't do something she obviously enjoyed. As the men cleaned up from their impromptu party, she sat next to the petite blonde.

"Thanks. I put my bathing suit on under my dress. Actually, it's just a sports bra and shorts, but it's the closest thing I had. I also wanted to apologize for spoiling your fun."

"It's okay. I'm so fat, I probably wouldn't be able to hang on to the rope anyway." Chelsea smiled and patted her tummy. "Well, not fat, but you know, pregnant. Tennyson would spank my backside if he heard me call myself that."

Thankfully, Zinnia had enough sense not to do a wellness check like she'd done with Jennifer. It was obvious their husbands shared the same proclivities. Her face warmed, but not entirely from embarrassment as she was reminded of the conversation. It made her wonder about things she had no business thinking about.

Like, how Mitch's hand would feel on her butt.

She wasn't entirely innocent. She'd had very imaginative boyfriends before Afghanistan, and at one time, had an e-reader full of naughty stories featuring domestic discipline and spanking. They were still in her account, which shockingly enough, hadn't gotten shut down, but she hadn't downloaded anything to her new device except medical reference texts.

"I almost forgot," Jennifer said, sitting next to them. "I sent you a copy of that book I was telling you about, Chelsea."

"Which one?" Chelsea asked.

"The one with the aliens using romance novels to choose mates."

"Wait. You mean the one where the aliens think romance books are relationship manuals?" Zinnia asked. It had been one of her favorites, and she wondered if the authors had ever written a second.

"Yes!" Jennifer sprang from her seat and grabbed her handbag, then pulled out an e-reader. "It's this one."

She turned the device to show Zinnia, but it didn't look familiar. "Did the authors change the cover? I don't remember that one."

Jennifer paled, then looked down. "I'm sorry. I... that was the third one."

There was a part of Zinnia that wanted to hide in her bed and cry for all the missed time, but she wasn't going to do that anymore. This was a good thing. It meant she could read those stories all over again and remember why she loved them.

"No, don't be sorry," she finally said. "You know what? This is the perfect opportunity to get my library loaded back up and start reading some dirty books."

"Kinky Bitches Book Club!" Chelsea replied, grinning. "Sunday brunch with mimosas once we deliver our babies."

"Where are we going to get brunch in Montgomery?" Jennifer asked. "We don't even have a Starbucks."

"Tennyson, of course. He's an excellent cook."

Chelsea put her hands on the arms of her chair and rocked, a clear signal to Zinnia that she wanted to stand and needed the momentum. "I don't know about you, but I want to get in the water."

"I'm looking forward to trying the rope swing," Zinnia replied. With Jennifer's help, they got Chelsea on her feet as the men came outside.

"Looks like you three are ready for a swim," Kaden said, giving his wife a soft smile.

Tennyson took over for Zinnia and helped Chelsea down the steps to a mulched pathway leading to a pergola next to the pond. Along with a large swing and several chairs with thick cushions, there was a freestanding firepit and citronella candles set on a round wooden table. Both dogs were already splashing in the shallows, looking like they were having a grand time chasing each other.

The setting sun cast a red glow over the pond, and she smiled when a fish jumped after an insect. "What kind of fish is that?"

"Rainbow trout," Mitch replied. "Tennyson stocks them. We usually catch and release, but they're delicious if you're in the mood for fish. There's poles and gear in the cottage."

"I've never been fishing, but I've had trout in restaurants before."

"Oh, no! We can't have that!" Chuckling, he pulled his shirt over his head, revealing a torso cut with muscles. Although he had very little body hair, a sweet treasure trail led into his jeans, making Zinnia resist the urge to lick her lips.

Pulling her out of her sensual haze, he added, "I'll show you how the rope swing works tonight, and you'll get your first fishing lesson tomorrow morning."

Zinnia pressed her lips together to keep her tongue from lolling out of her mouth as he unzipped his jeans and slid them down. He wore tight black swim trunks set low on his hipbones, revealing a chiseled Adonis belt.

"Dayum."

Chelsea nudged her arm and grinned, making her realize she'd spoken out loud. Thankfully, Mitch didn't hear.

After laying his clothes on the arm of an Adirondack chair, he said, "The water's a little chilly so you might want to get used to it first. Coming?"

Without waiting for an answer, he jogged to the water's edge and threw himself in with a yell.

"You better catch up before you miss your chance," Chelsea whispered in her ear.

"Chance for what? The swing will still be there."

"The chance to see what those shorts look like when they're wet."

"Shh!" Jennifer hustled them out of earshot of Kaden and Tennyson. "You're going to get us in trouble."

"I'm pregnant, not dead," Chelsea retorted. "And that is prime, grade-A eye candy."

"Preach, sister," Zinnia murmured, her eyes fixed on Mitch as he swam across the pond. Her fingers trembling, she untied the fabric belt of her dress, then pulled it over her head and toed off her sneakers.

Carefully tended by their husbands, Jennifer and Chelsea led the way to the small pea gravel beach. The ground under her feet was still warm from the sun, but slightly damp and spongy as if it had rained recently. The concrete covering all but a scant few pockets of green space in St. Louis had felt just like the stone of her cave. Dry and sterile, it didn't feed her soul.

This felt like... life.

She took a single step into the water, her toes curling at the chill. It was almost magical, and tears pricked her eyes when she remembered how close she'd come to never experiencing this miracle at all.

Mitch swam toward her, then stood and held out

his hand. Smiling at her, he said, "Come on in. The water's fine."

The breath left her body like she'd been punched in the stomach, and she forgot all about the cold water lapping at her feet. Blessed be, Chelsea had been right. Those swim trunks were surely a gift from the Goddess.

"Ahh! It's cold!"

Zinnia stood waist deep in the water. The contrast of her vivid yellow sports bra and shorts against her mahogany skin made him smile. Mitch loved that she was comfortable enough to wear bright colors. It meant she wasn't trying to hide.

She was thin, although he didn't know if it was because of lingering malnutrition or if she was at her usual body weight. He hoped it was the latter, but it wasn't his place to ask. He wasn't anything to her.

*Not yet, but you could be.*

He shook the random thought away and tried not to lick his lips when her nipples hardened under the thin fabric of her sports bra. Thankfully, the water was cold enough to convince his cock to behave itself. He had no desire to sport wood in front of her and all his friends.

"You'll get used to it," he said. "Just take that first step."

"I'm gonna hate myself in the morning," she muttered, closing her eyes. Without warning, she threw herself into the water. She came up sputtering, her eyes wide with shock.

"Are you okay?" he asked, hurrying to her side. Water trickled over her skin, the droplets glistening in the sunlight as she brushed wavy strands of wet hair out of her face.

"I almost squashed a fish!" She burst into laughter as goosebumps erupted on her arms. "How the heck did it miss a six-foot-tall woman falling out of the sky?"

Chuckling, he led her deeper into the water. "I forgot to ask if you could swim."

"Yeah, I mean, I took lessons when I was a kid."

"I'll make sure you don't drown."

To his shock, she leaned forward and kissed him. It was almost chaste, yet it seemed as if her mouth branded him. Searing heat coursed down his spine, and he forced his hands to stay where they were. Mitch wanted nothing more than to pull her into his arms and deepen their kiss, but he didn't want to frighten her. Aside from that, they didn't have a future together. She was meant for bigger and better things—not a retired soldier almost fifteen years her senior.

In a desperate attempt to quell his rising attraction, he said, "Ready to try the rope swing?"

"More than ready. Where is it?"

He pointed across the pond at the rope hanging from the sturdy branch of an old maple tree above an elevated platform. "Can you swim that far?"

"Maybe? Might as well find out."

She set off, but he caught up to her awkward dog-paddle easily. "If you get tired, move closer to shore. The pond is about fifteen feet deep in the middle, but it's shallow enough to wade closer to the bank."

Although she was breathing hard, they soon made it to the small platform. Normally used for fishing, it had railing on three sides with an open section facing the pond. The knotted rope swing was tied around one of the posts.

She climbed the few steps and rested her elbows on the railing. "Whew! I did it!"

Mitch smiled at the look of pride on her face and untied the rope, checking to make sure it was sound.

"You sure did. Rest for a second to make sure you can swim back."

"I should have listened to my doctor when he told me to get to the gym," she muttered, laying a hand on her chest. "I'm so out of shape."

His palm itched to paddle her bottom for ignoring her doctor's orders. It was none of his business, but he had to know. "Why didn't you?"

Zinnia frowned and looked out over the water. "It's not a very good excuse, but there were too many people and I... anyway, how do I use this thing?"

He let her change the subject without comment. "Grab the rope above the knot, get a running start, and jump. Let go when you're out over the water."

"That's it?"

"Yep. Want me to show you?"

"Please."

He hid a smile at the look of relief in Zinnia's eyes. She was trying so hard to be brave.

"Okay. Watch where I land. That's where the water is the deepest." He reached for the rope, showing her where to hold on, then ran forward a few steps and jumped. After surfacing, he swam back, noticing she'd already caught the swing. "Your turn," he called.

"Will the fish bite me if I land on them again?"

"No, baby girl. They only eat insects." He swam closer to the platform and watched her shift her feet nervously. "Do you want to me to go with you? You can ride piggyback."

Her expressive face revealed her indecision, but she shook her head. "I can do it."

Despite her words, she didn't move. He frowned and got out of the water, meaning to help her. Before he reached the stairs, she raced to the end of the platform and jumped. Screaming in a mix of terror and joy, she swung out over the deep part of the pond and let go, then pulled her long limbs into a cannonball and landed with a tremendous splash.

She rose to the surface and sputtered as she paddled awkwardly to keep her head above water. "I did it! Did you see, Daddy?"

His lungs seized at the address, and at the appalled expression on her face. He had to tell himself over and over that she hadn't meant it. It was nothing more than excitement, and she didn't understand the reference. He swallowed the ache in his chest and said, "You sure did, Zinnia. Good girl."

# CHAPTER 7

*Idiot!*

What the heck was wrong with her? Zinnia had no idea what made her call him Daddy. The mix of horror and shock on Mitch's face almost made her want to drown herself in the pond. As it was, she ducked her head under the water to cool the heat rising in her cheeks. Could she have made things more awkward?

"Do you need help getting to shore?" he asked, his expression settling into an emotionless mask.

Smoothing her face into what she hoped was a pleasant, not at all mortified expression, she said, "No, you go on. I'll just take my time and move to the shallows if I get tired."

"Are you sure? I don't know—"

"I'll be okay. I just… can you give me a minute?" She silently begged him to leave her alone so she could suffer her humiliation in peace.

Although he looked worried, he nodded. "All right. I'll watch for you, just in case."

"Thanks."

He set off for shore and she resisted the urge to slap herself upside the head. She blamed Chelsea and Jennifer. It was all their fault for reminding her of all those happy-ever-afters she used to read and once dreamed of for herself.

Thank the Goddess no one else heard her.

*Mitch called you his baby girl. There's nothing wrong with calling him Daddy in return.*

Zinnia spun in place, sure she'd heard a woman's husky voice whispering behind her, but no one was there. She was at least thirty yards from shore, meaning it couldn't have been Chelsea or Jennifer either. Maybe it was the Goddess, but…

"I'm probably hearing things, but girlfriend, you need to mind your own self. My love life is not your business."

Although she thought she'd gotten used to the chilly water, her poor body condition meant it took ages to paddle back to shore and she was shivering by the time she got out. Mitch was waiting for her with a giant beach towel and wrapped it around her shoulders as she trudged up the sloped bank.

"You're cold." Mitch led her to a chair next to the fire pit. "I should have helped you."

"I'm okay." Zinnia leaned forward, soaking up the heat.

"Want a s'more?" Chelsea asked. "We found you a stick. It's with the marshmallows and chocolate."

"Yes, please." Holding her towel closed, she grabbed the stick and Mitch stuck a marshmallow on it. She laughed softly, then added, "I've never toasted a marshmallow before."

"At the risk of being insulting, how did you make it to thirty without toasting a marshmallow?" Jennifer asked.

*Good question.*

"I grew up in the city, and my parents' idea of roughing-it was the Four Seasons."

"You sound like the Prince of Posh." Jennifer giggled and bumped Kaden's shoulder.

"Watch it, little girl," Kaden warned. Despite his words, he gave Jennifer a fond smile and kissed her knuckles.

They were so danged cute together. Zinnia sighed, wishing for... Heck, she didn't know what she wanted. She wasn't ready to get into a relation-ship at all but couldn't help a tiny surge of jealousy.

"Just hold the marshmallow above the flames until it gets brown," Mitch said, helping her position the stick. "Keep turning it so it doesn't melt and fall into the fire."

"Or you can let it catch on fire. Tennyson likes them burnt," Chelsea added. "We have plenty of marshmallows so you can figure out how you like them."

"Probably not burnt. More golden brown like the top of a crème brûlée."

"Finally! Someone with taste!" Kaden said.

Everyone laughed at him, but it made Zinnia feel somewhat uncomfortable. This was her new home, and she was beginning to love it, yet she didn't quite fit in. She was from the city, and everything here was completely new to her, but she was determined to adapt. Straightening her spine, she spun her marshmallow to toast the other side. After all, she'd learned two new things today—she loved swinging from a rope and toasting marshmallows over a campfire. And tomorrow, Mitch would teach her how to catch a fish—not that she'd know what to do with it once she had it.

*Baby steps, Zinnia.* Besides, after her verbal faux

pas, it wouldn't surprise her if he wanted nothing to do with her.

Then again, he *had* called her baby girl…

No. It was just an idiom folks up here used. The old man at the last sugar shack she stopped at on her way had called her that too, but she'd thought nothing of it at the time. He had to have been eighty if he was a day—everyone was probably a baby to him.

"Your marshmallow is melting," Mitch said, interrupting her reverie.

"Oh, thanks. What do I do now?"

"Here." He handed her a plate with graham crackers and a square of chocolate laid out. "Use the cracker to scrape the marshmallow onto the chocolate, then make a sandwich with it."

"Got it." Carefully, she assembled the treat, then took a bite. The marshmallow melted the chocolate into a sticky, wonderful mess and she moaned in pleasure. "Blessed be, that's delicious."

"You can roast hot dogs over the fire too," Chelsea said. "We even have a grate for fish."

"My favorite is dripping maple syrup on snow, then rolling it onto a stick like a popsicle," Jennifer said. "But we'll have to wait until late October for that."

"I could make up a mess of barbecued ribs," Zinnia said, wanting to contribute something she actually knew how to do. She also wasn't sure she wanted to think about snow happening in October. "Low Country potato salad, corn on the cob, greens, and a gooey butter cake."

"Stop!" Chelsea laid a hand over her stomach and groaned. "I just ate my weight in pizza and birthday cake, and now I'm hungry again."

"What's a gooey butter cake?" Tennyson asked. "Sounds delicious."

"It's a St. Louis specialty with a whole box of powdered sugar, cream cheese, and—"

"Daddy, make her stop." Chelsea covered her face, then peeked at Zinnia through her fingers. "Can we do that next weekend?"

"Sure! I need to—" Without warning, Zinnia yawned. "I'm so sorry. It's been a long couple of days."

Mitch stood and helped her up. "Let's get you inside. It's getting dark, and the bugs are starting to come out anyway."

"We're heading home too," Kaden said. "Jennifer has the early shift at the clinic tomorrow and I'm going to Costco in Colchester."

Tennyson pulled out his phone. "That reminds me. I forgot to send you our list."

Kaden's phone chimed, and he glanced at Zinnia. "If you have a shopping list, I can take care of it while I'm there."

"Oh, I don't want to put you out. I can—"

"Little girl, it's an hour's drive one way," he interrupted. "Besides, it will be your turn next month."

Little girl, baby girl. The diminutives would have sent past Zinnia into a feminist rage. They didn't bother her coming from Mitch and his friends though. Maybe they should have, but they made her feel warm and cared for.

Protected.

"I... okay. I'll put one together tonight and text it to you." After handing him her phone, she added, "I just need your number."

Sooner or later, she'd have to check her messages. If nothing else, Zinnia needed to let everyone know she'd arrived safely, yet she was enjoying herself too much to risk ruining it.

Chelsea yawned and struggled to stand. "Don't forget the ingredients for gooey butter cake."

"And I've never had homemade barbecued ribs." Jennifer leaned against Kaden's chest and wrapped her arms around his waist. "Or Low Country potato salad."

"What's the difference between Low Country potato salad and regular potato salad?" Mitch asked.

"Old Bay, shrimp, and andouille sausage. At least, that's how my aunt always made it." Zinnia gave Caleb's ears one last scritch, then kissed his furry head, wishing she had the nerve to ask Jennifer if she could keep him.

Jennifer sighed, then reached up to tug Kaden's hair. "If you don't buy all the things on her list, I'm going to strap you to the cross."

"If I forget, I'll let you. Ready to go?"

"Good night!" Zinnia called after them. After the conversations she'd had with Jennifer and Chelsea, she had a pretty good idea what kind of cross they were talking about but decided not to mention it.

Tennyson cleaned up the remaining marshmallows and chocolate, then whistled for Princess. "I'm putting my little girls to bed. Zinnia, Mitch will help you, but text me if you need anything, okay?"

"Yes, thank you. I'll be fine."

She slipped on her shoes as they walked away, then grabbed her dress. It had gotten dark so quickly, almost without her realizing it. It wasn't until Mitch extinguished their fire with a few buckets of water that she noticed.

It wasn't completely dark like her cave had been though. The stars gleamed silver and a crescent moon hung low in the sky. Instead of silence punctuated by shouts and occasional gunfire or the constant thrum of inescapable traffic noise, frogs and crickets sang their evening melody.

Maybe the absence of city noise should have disturbed her, but she didn't miss it a single bit.

"Talk to me, Zinnia."

The sound of a human voice made her flinch. "Huh?"

Mitch offered her his arm, then said, "Sorry I startled you. I just wanted you to keep up a conversation. There are bears in the woods, and the noise keeps them away."

"Really? That's..." She chuckled and took his arm, allowing him to escort her back to the cottage. "I have no idea why I'm surprised."

They reached the cottage and Mitch held the door for her. After wiping her feet, she stepped inside and took off her sneakers.

"You don't need to worry too much about them. Just make sure to use the bear-resistant cans for your trash and lock your car. I can take care of it if you didn't."

"It's locked but thank you. In St. Louis, it was car thieves instead of bears."

He laughed softly and followed her toward the bedrooms. "You can have the bathroom first. If you want some, I can make us some hot chocolate."

"No, thanks. You can go first in the bathroom too. I kind of want to soak in that tub. It's been an age since I've seen one big enough for me to stretch out."

"Well, since you put it that way…" As much as he wanted to see her needs met, he didn't want her to feel rushed. "I won't be long."

"Great. I'll start unpacking."

He stared after her as she walked into her bedroom, watching the play of silky fabric over a seriously magnificent backside. That was one thing the photos he'd obsessed over hadn't shown, and he wouldn't mind looking at it for…

Mitch cut the thought off before it went any further. He wasn't going to be around to watch any of her. Instead of lamenting what couldn't ever be, he grabbed his toiletries bag and a change of clothes, then undressed and stepped under the shower.

His cock thickened, swelling as he bathed, and the image of water trickling down Zinnia's long limbs like falling diamonds in the sunlight filled his mind's eye, inescapable and compelling. Letting out a groan, he squeezed his eyes shut and banished the memory.

Zinnia was a person, damaged, but strong enough to recreate her life. He had no business jacking off while thinking about her. Too bad his cock didn't seem to be getting the memo. Eventually, he softened, allowing him to finish up and get dressed in a T-shirt and sweats.

"Bathroom's all yours," he called, tapping on the doorframe leading into her bedroom.

"Thanks." She slid a stack of folded clothing into a dresser drawer, then turned. "And thanks again for staying with me."

"No problem." He took a step inside and caught a whiff of her citrus and sunshine perfume as he maneuvered around a stack of boxes. "Do you want some help unpacking?"

"Actually, about half this stuff is going to my new office." She grimaced, then gave him a shamefaced smile. "You and Kaden moved all these books, and it didn't occur to me to have you leave them in my car."

"There was a lot going on. And Jennifer was feeding you wine at the time. I'll help you tomorrow."

"No, it's okay. I'll just—"

"Zinnia, stop." His voice deepened, softer but no less stern. It was the tone he used for disobedient submissives, meant to encourage them to make good choices. "I don't want to catch you moving those boxes by yourself."

She blinked, then her eyes narrowed. "Seems to me I loaded them just fine without help when I packed up to move here."

Mitch had to remind himself she wasn't his sub and had no reason to obey. Yet his fists tightened with irritation. It had been a long time since anyone had disobeyed him. Forcibly calming himself, he let his hands relax.

Before he could apologize, she added, "Who made you the boss of me anyway?"

She was baiting him, but he wasn't about to let the challenge go unanswered. "You did, baby girl. The minute you asked me to stay with you."

"I—"

"So, here's what's going to happen. You're going

to take a long, hot bath and get a good night's sleep. I will help you move everything tomorrow. If you decide to disobey, there will be consequences."

"You can leave any time." She lifted her chin imperiously and turned away. "I just wanted some company. Not a bossy—"

Before he could stop himself, he swatted her ass hard.

"Ouch!" She spun and rubbed her bottom, her eyes sparking with anger. "What the hell was that for?"

"Consequences, Zinnia." He let out a breath and tried to stifle the urge to turn her over his knee for a more thorough spanking. She wasn't ready, and he shouldn't have spanked her in the first place, but he wasn't about to let her do everything herself when she was still recovering from her captivity. "Let me take care of you, please."

"I... shit." Her jaw worked and she looked down, but not quickly enough for him to miss the glint of tears in her eyes.

"Oh, sweetheart." Slowly, as if she was made of glass, he pulled her into a hug. "It's going to be okay."

Sniffing, she buried her face in the crook of his neck as the tension eased from her spine. "I'm not okay."

"I know, but every day will get a little better, and you'll eventually be more okay than you are right now."

"When?" She wriggled closer and tightened her arms around him as if she was afraid he'd let go.

"Good question. I can't answer it for you, but it's okay to not be okay."

She lifted her head and backed away, then scrubbed at her eyes with the back of her hand. "Aside from my therapist, you're the first person to tell me that. My own cousin asked me if I was off my meds because I gagged when I tried to eat rice. It was like a joke to him."

He made a note to punch her cousin in the face. "Triggering?" he finally asked.

"That was all I ate for over a year. I can't even stand the smell of it." She barked out a laugh and shook her head. "I lost it over my aunt's dirty rice. Spicy enough to make your eyes water with bits of sausage and peppers, and a little bacon grease for flavor. I used to love it."

Sighing, she unwrapped her hair and tried for a smile. "Just a day in the life of a PTSD patient, right?"

Mitch resisted the urge to pull her into another hug. He'd grown up eating rice with almost every meal, but no one in his family would have been so insensitive. "Don't make it with rice. Use... I don't know. Couscous?"

She studied him for a moment, then scowled. "I could seriously almost hate you, you know?"

"Why?"

She balled up the damp fabric and tossed it at his head. "Couscous? Really?"

"It was just a thought." He caught the towel and put it in the hamper. People were sometimes funny about those old family recipes. For all he knew, suggesting a change would start a generations-long feud.

"No, sir. It is not just a thought." Still scowling, she stomped to him and laid her palms on his cheeks, then kissed him full on the mouth.

Her tongue demanded entry and he groaned, pulling her closer as she put one hand on the back of his head to hold him still. As much as he wanted to give her space, he just... couldn't.

How the hell was he supposed to let her go now that he had her? She was alive and safe, and kissing him like there was no tomorrow.

He nipped her lower lip, then soothed the sting with the tip of his tongue as he cupped her perfect ass in his palms. The scent of her faded perfume filled his senses, growing stronger as he claimed her mouth.

The soft sound of a needy whimper brought him out of his aroused fugue, and he softened his touch, allowing her to pull away even though every cell in his body demanded he never let her go.

She blinked back tears and touched her swollen lips, then cleared her throat. "I... Mitch, you didn't give me a thought. You gave me hope."

# CHAPTER 8

Zinnia could barely meet Mitch's eyes after kissing the shit out of him.

Over couscous, of all things. What the hell was wrong with her? And after she'd waved her triggers and insecurities around like someone tossing beads at a Mardi Gras parade.

*Where's a hole I can bury myself in?*

He touched her shoulder, making her look at him, then gave her an easy smile. "Kind of like an adaptation, you know? If rice doesn't work for you, find something that does."

"Maybe."

"Add the ingredients to your grocery list. I'll be your taste tester."

"Sure." She chewed on her lip, wondering what to do with her hands.

The same hands that had touched Mitch like she owned him. Or something.

*He wasn't exactly protesting, baby girl.*

"Shut up!"

"Excuse me?" Mitch arched a brow, then crossed his arms over his chest. The fabric stretched tight over his muscular shoulders, and she nearly lost her train of thought.

"Sorry! I'm so sorry. I was talking to myself, not you." Without looking, she grabbed her toiletries bag and a robe, then scurried around him to escape into the bathroom.

She closed the door, careful not to slam it, then slumped against it. "Goddess, I'm a hot mess," she muttered. "Emphasis on the mess. Nothing good ever comes from hearing strange voices."

After stoppering the tub, she adjusted the taps until the water was the perfect temperature, then looked through her collection of essential oils. Hopefully, one of them would help soothe her scattered, mixed-up mind.

Lavender, vanilla, clary sage, jasmine... No, definitely not jasmine. She eventually chose sage and rosemary, hoping the slightly astringent scents would give her clarity, then tipped a few drops of each into the bath.

She dropped her clothes into a heap on the floor before stepping into the steaming water. The tub was deep, the lip coming almost to her shoulder when she sat, and more than long enough to stretch out.

Sheer bliss.

Before she forgot, Zinnia typed up her grocery list and texted it to Kaden, then without reading the dozens of texts from her family, sent one to her mother saying she was safe. After that was done, she washed the pond water from her hair. Using a rolled towel as a pillow, she let the warm water soothe her anxious mind and tense body until the bath cooled, which took a surprisingly long time. Then again, she'd been soaking in a giant cast-iron pot for almost an hour, doing her best impression of her New Orleans-bred grandmother's crawfish boil.

Her joints feeling like rubber, she staggered from the tub and dried off, barely able to keep her eyes open. Hell, it was work just putting on her robe.

Unfortunately, she wasn't too tired to think about the one thing she'd almost but not quite pushed from her mind. That single spank Mitch had given her. Her butt still twitched and burned from the phantom sting.

It hadn't hurt much, yet the sensation remained long after the event. What would have happened if he'd continued? She had no idea if she'd like it or hate it, and she certainly wasn't going to ask for a demonstration—no matter how much reading about it revved her motor. Well, it used to anyway.

Maybe there was some chance of him being into it. After all, he was friends with Kaden and Tennyson, and according to their wives, they were very much fans.

She couldn't ask him though. What man like that would want a woman like... her? She was about half crazy, couldn't sleep without a nightlight—when she could sleep at all—and melted down over a fucking plate of rice.

Every bit of calm she'd managed to gather while bathing vanished like she hadn't even tried. She scrubbed at her eyes and let out a slow breath.

"Damn it."

Mitch tapped on the door, making her flinch and peek in the mirror to make sure she didn't look like she was about to cry again.

"Hey, you okay in there?"

"I'm good," she replied, opening the door. "Just finished getting ready for bed."

"Good." He gazed at her for a moment, then appeared to shake himself. "Great. See you in the morning?"

"Yeah." Zinnia turned toward her room, then stole a quick glance back. "Thanks for teaching me to use the rope swing."

"We'll do fishing tomorrow."

"Sounds like fun." Despite her intent, her feet wouldn't move. She wanted… crap, she didn't even know what she wanted. She forced herself to put one foot after the other until she reached her bedroom.

"We'll catch one for lunch," he promised. "But one more thing before you go to sleep."

"What's that?"

He moved into her space, letting her feel his body heat against her skin. "I want you to agree to the consequences if you don't let me take care of you."

"I…" She chewed her lip, then nodded. Maybe this would be a chance to see what all the fuss was about in her naughty books without putting herself at risk. She trusted Mitch, for all that she'd known him for less than a day. Aside from that, he'd be leaving soon, meaning there wouldn't be any lingering awkwardness. "Okay."

"Good girl." He brushed a kiss over her cheek. "Good night, Zinnia."

"Night!" She closed the door, then knocked her head against the wood a few times. "Goddess, I'm an idiot."

Letting out a tired sigh, she trudged to the bed and set up her nightlight, then turned on the white noise app on her phone. Instead of reaching for her aromatherapy diffuser, she opened both windows to allow the evening breeze into the room.

Zinnia inhaled deeply and closed her eyes, smelling trees and honeysuckle, a faint hint of algae from the pond, and fresh, clean air. Insects and bull-frogs provided a nicer bedtime melody than her white noise app, so she turned it off. She tossed her robe on a chair and got into bed wearing just her panties. Cool bamboo sheets caressed her skin and she let out a little moan of pleasure.

The brilliant crescent moon sent faint illumination into the room, and she almost considered unplugging her nightlight too.

Almost.

She rolled over and punched her pillow, then bent her knees so her feet didn't hang over the edge.

Even with a nightlight, there was no sense tempting fate or the monsters under the bed.

ZINNIA WAS TUCKED in and safe. Why, then, couldn't Mitch sleep?

He tried to tell himself it was because the woman he'd dreamed about for years was only a few feet away, and he'd finally be able to spend time getting to know the person behind the photographs and cheerful social media posts.

It was really that breath-stealing kiss. He still tasted her on his lips, and he'd have given his left nut to do it again. Closing his eyes, his cock hardened as he imagined her under the dim illumination of Saints and Sinners' suspension area. Her long limbs and luscious curves just begged to be tied, and she'd be glorious in brightly colored hemp rope.

Mitch bit off an ugly curse and pushed the image away. Zinnia was definitely not ready for that, and he felt like the worst kind of predator for even thinking about it. It was bad enough he'd almost forced her to agree to let him take care of her.

Someone needed to though, and he wasn't about to let anyone else do it. She needed to know she was safe and people cared about her. He promised himself he'd ease back when she lost the ever-present pinched expression of anxiety she displayed.

He sat up and rubbed his face, then walked to the window and leaned on the wide sill. The cool night air soothed him, and he caught the faint odor of morning glories from the planter hung just outside, but he shivered. He still hadn't gotten used to how dark it was out here without ambient light from a nearby city or even a streetlight. Then again, he supposed he'd become accustomed to it if he lived here for more than a few weeks.

Straightening, he glanced toward Zinnia's room. She'd spent over a year in the dark. Mitch was halfway down the hall before he realized he'd even moved, wearing nothing but boxer briefs.

"She's fine," he muttered to himself as he trudged back to his bed. At least she hadn't seen him barreling toward her like a crazy man. It would have scared the crap out of her.

Still, it wouldn't hurt to check on her—just to be sure. He put on his discarded sweats and crept to her room, then opened her door as quietly as he could. A nightlight cast faint illumination and his heart squeezed uncomfortably at the sight of her curled on her side in a tight ball with the sheets tucked to her chin.

Without warning, the bulb in the nightlight went out with a barely audible pop and plunged the room into stygian darkness. As if she'd heard it, Zinnia whimpered softly, her terror palpable even in sleep.

"Oh, damn, baby girl," he whispered, taking a step into her room. "It's okay."

His vision adjusted to the faint starlight, and he let out another soft curse as she shuddered. Her breathing sped up and he crossed the room, then let his hand hover over her shoulder.

His touch might give her comfort, but it could just as easily send her into a panic attack.

"Zinnia, honey, you're okay," he said, keeping his tone soft and encouraging.

She woke with a tearing scream and her arms flailed as she struggled free of the sheets. The bedside lamp tumbled to the floor and the resulting crash sent her scrabbling across the bed to land on the floor.

"It's okay!" he called, then whirled to slap at the light switch in the hall. "Your nightlight went out, baby girl. I turned on the hall light for you."

Zinnia peeked above the edge of the bed, her

eyes wide with fear. Within seconds, they cleared as she woke up fully and she blew out a relieved sigh.

"Fuck's sake," she muttered under her breath. Lifting her head, she tried for a smile. "I'm so sorry to have woken you."

Normally, Mitch would have chided her for her language, yet the frustration in her voice stopped him. She slumped wearily, her arms coming up to fold under her head, and he wondered when her last full night's sleep had been.

"You didn't." He grabbed her robe from the chair and laid it within reach. "I was up and decided to check on you."

"Um… thanks." She wriggled into the robe and stood, then gave him a weak smile. "I'm not going to get back to sleep, so I'll go sit in the living room and read. Don't worry about the lamp. I'll clean it up tomorrow."

He set the lamp back on the table. The bulb wasn't broken, but he unplugged it, meaning to check it in the morning.

"Nope." He held out a hand. "You can sleep in the bigger room. I'll leave the hall light on and stay with you so you can get a good night's rest."

She frowned, then shook her head. "No, I'm fine.

You go on back to bed and I'll see you in the morning."

"Baby girl, do you remember what I said about consequences?" He took her hand, then led her into the larger of the two bedrooms.

"I don't believe stealing your bed counts. Where are you going to sleep?"

"Next to you with a pillow between us. The bed is plenty big enough." He threw back the sheets and pointed. "Now, in you go."

Mitch almost thought he saw a flicker of heat in her dark brown eyes, but she folded her arms across her chest, shook her head again, then tried to step around him.

"I'll be fine on the couch."

"Last warning, sweetheart. You're going to rest, and I'll stay right here to keep you safe."

"No. I'm—"

He caught her around the waist and sat on the edge of the bed, then pulled her down over his lap. "Your consequence tonight is five spanks."

"What? No!" She struggled, nearly sliding from his lap, but he kept her in place easily with a hand around her waist.

Mitch knew he was taking a risk, but he couldn't watch her struggle anymore. It was time for her to let him carry some of the weight—as he hadn't been able to do in Afghanistan.

"You agreed to the consequences if you didn't let me take care of you," he replied quietly. "You can say red if it's too much, but this is going to happen."

# CHAPTER 9

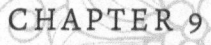

*B*ack when Zinnia still had hope her parents would let her have a pet, she'd read that kittens relaxed and went limp when their mamas carried them by the back of the neck. She imagined laying over Mitch's lap was like that. She wasn't even worried about the five spanks he'd promised her.

Well, not too worried.

She trusted him and knew deep in her soul that he wouldn't hurt her. In fact, the only thing that truly concerned her was that she'd like it.

Her collection of erotic novels had never been enough. She'd been able to imagine it and often touched herself while fantasizing about a strong, handsome man taking her over his knee, but had no practical experience.

More than that, she felt… safe. Like he actually cared enough to call her on her bullshit. He wasn't going to let her pretend to be okay when she wasn't, but he was willing to give her a chance to try things herself.

Like with the rope swing. He'd have been happy to carry her but was equally pleased to let her try. She almost wished she'd let him help her back to shore, but he'd watched her like a hawk to make sure she didn't drown her crazy-ass self.

There was overwhelming freedom and security in knowing she didn't have to hide anymore. He saw everything she'd concealed for two years and didn't judge her for it.

"Zinnia, honey, do you understand? Say red if it's too much."

The words pulled her from her thoughts but didn't startle her. "Yes… Daddy, I understand."

Unlike when she'd called him that after going on the rope swing, the honorific came out smoothly and she didn't second-guess herself. Mitch was a Daddy, like Kaden and Tennyson. Maybe he wouldn't be around for long, but he could be hers for the time she had him.

He leaned down and kissed the back of her neck. "There's my good girl. Five spanks, then it will be over, and we'll have a good night's sleep."

She braced her hands against his leg and let out a breath, her body relaxing over his lap. Maybe she had no idea what she was in for, but there was freedom in that too. It was the first time since her rescue that she hadn't panicked over a new experience.

*Slap!*

The first spank came without warning and stung bad enough to steal her breath even through her panties and robe. Mitch followed up with four more, two on each butt cheek. They melded together in a wave of sensation that didn't exactly hurt.

He petted her backside to soothe the sting, then helped her sit up in his lap as he crooned a soft melody in a minor key that reminded her of wind chimes.

"All done, baby girl. I'm so proud of you." He held her tight, gently encouraging her to rest her head on his shoulder. "Such a good girl."

Tears burned in her eyes, and she sniffed, but not because she was in pain.

Zinnia's captors hadn't left her completely unscathed. There had been punches, slaps, the occasional kick, and they hadn't been shy about pushing her around.

Maybe a normal woman would have compared the abuse she'd suffered to being spanked, but it wasn't the same at all. Her captors had treated her like a beast of burden, using the threat of physical violence to keep her obedient. It hadn't been personal, nor had they gone out of their way to hurt her if she did as she was told. In fact, they rarely came near her at all unless one of them needed medical attention.

But this... Mitch's spanking had been incredibly intimate and the feel of his warm, bare skin against her cheek set her nerve endings alight. He held her and kept humming that repetitive melody like a lullaby as if he tried to soothe her. She wished she had the nerve to ask him to spank her again but didn't want him to let her go.

For the first time in years, she was at peace. Her mind was quiet, and her heart didn't feel like it was going to leap from her chest. The dark didn't scare her anymore. Well, not while she was sitting on Mitch's lap, at least. She buried her nose in the crook of his neck and drew the faint scent of jasmine and male musk into her lungs as the heat from her freshly spanked bottom moved into her core.

Mitch tightened his arms around her, then kissed her temple. "Are you okay, baby girl? Talk to me."

She lifted her head and leaned back slightly to look into his warm brown eyes. "Never better."

As it was easier to ask forgiveness than permission, she kissed him before he could tell her no.

A low rumble vibrated his chest, and he pulled her close as he deepened their kiss, stealing her breath along with her wits. He tasted warm and spicy, and his lips were firm on hers, yet almost painfully gentle too. The tip of his tongue slicked a decadent trail across her lower lip, then he nipped her.

"Goddess!"

He pulled back, then chuckled softly when she whined and tried to keep him close. "Naughty," he murmured softly, then tapped her nose.

"Tease." She turned to straddle his lap, but somehow, he managed to maneuver her to sit on the bed next to him.

"I'm going to hate myself forever for this." His shoulders slumped, then he turned and gave her a wry smile. "But we have to stop, honey."

"You said you'd give me everything I needed," she countered. "And I kind of need... you."

"Zinnia, I—" He cut himself off and gazed at her for several seconds, indecision coloring his features.

It took a minute for her to understand what he was trying not to say and her face burned with a blush he thankfully couldn't see. What the heck was wrong with her? She'd all but attacked him, and he clearly wasn't interested in her like that.

"No, you're right. I'm sorry." She jumped to her feet and tightened the sash of her robe, needing something to do with her hands. "I just... it's fine. I'm going back to my room."

And then she'd delete every one of those damned romance books before they gave her more ideas about getting a happy ever after.

THE TINY FLASH of hurt disappointment in her eyes vanished almost as quickly as it appeared, leaving Mitch feeling like an asshole.

Making love to Zinnia would have been a dream come true, but he couldn't let it happen. Hell, he was almost old enough to be her father in truth—not just her Daddy.

He'd played with younger women many times, yet never with the same one more than once or twice. Of course, none of those partners had been Zinnia—the one woman he wanted for more than a casual scene. If they made love, he wasn't sure he'd ever be able to let her go.

"I'm sorry," she said when he didn't answer right away. "I thought we... anyway, I'll be fine."

He caught her wrist gently before she could escape. "I'd like nothing better than to make love to you until you fall unconscious, but I'm fifteen years older than you are."

"I think that stops mattering so much when we're both over thirty," she murmured, extricating her wrist from his grasp. "And you don't need to give me excuses. Consent is a yes or no question and it goes both ways. You're not required to provide a reason for either answer."

It was more than clear she understood how consent worked. She also wasn't a college student hooking up with an older instructor. Zinnia was a grown woman, and Mitch had no business telling her what she should or shouldn't want.

Maybe there was a way to make her change her mind. He hesitated, then decided it was for the best.

There was no way she was ready for what he really wanted from her.

"You're right about consent," he finally said, "but I do want to give you a reason."

"That isn't necessary." She turned to face the door, but he caught her hand before she could escape.

"Your consent is only the first thing I want from you." He stood and crowded her against the bed, shamelessly getting into her space.

She swallowed nervously and her lips parted on a soft gasp. "What else do you want?"

He traced a finger down her breastbone and nudged the collar of her robe aside to reveal the upper curve of her breast. "Everything, little girl."

"I... what does that mean?"

"Just what it sounds like." Gently, he turned her to face the window and standing behind her, he circled her elegant throat with his hand. Her breath hitched and he felt her pulse race under his fingertips.

To his surprise, she leaned against him, putting her ear in just the right position to nip. "You'll have to be more specific. *Everything* covers a lot of ground."

Mitch couldn't decide if he was proud of her for

holding her ground or disappointed she wasn't already halfway to Connecticut. He'd need to up his game to convince her he wasn't the right person for her.

"I'd start by tying you with rope." Unable to resist the urge to taste her, he bit her earlobe, then licked it to soothe the sting. "But not just to hold you still. I'd want to make something beautiful."

"Shibari? That's what it's called, right?"

"Sounds like someone's done some research." He moved his hand down her breastbone to untie the sash of her robe, then pulled it free of the loops. "I'd tie you into a corset, then a chastity belt with a knot right over your pretty little clit. You'd feel it every time you moved, and it would make you beg to come."

To his surprise, she let out a soft whimper and her head fell back against his shoulder. "Like the harness you tied around me when—"

"Yes, just like that." He wanted to warn her away from him—not remind her of her captivity. Considering he'd been the one to rescue her, he'd probably always make her think of how long she'd spent in that cave before he managed to find her. It was just one more reason to keep his hands to himself.

Not that he needed another.

"It felt like a hug."

Her whisper had been so soft, he wondered if he'd been meant to hear the words. "Then I want to suspend you. You'd be trapped, floating through the air with only the rope to hold you up."

She turned to face him and swallowed, then licked her bottom lip. "Then what?"

He closed his eyes and choked back a groan of need, his cock swelling. It was more than clear his plan had backfired, but he couldn't find it within himself to be disappointed. He took her wrist and wound the sash around it, then captured the other. When her hands were secure, he pushed the robe from her shoulders, leaving her bare to him and trapped in the silky fabric.

"Then I want to tease you until you beg me to let you come. I want to drip hot wax all over your gorgeous body, then cool the sting with ice. After that, I'll bind you to a spanking bench and give you the fun kind of spanking that makes you so desperate for relief you'll beg again."

He stopped before he told her he wanted to wrap her in rope so she could never leave him. Thankfully, he managed to keep that part to himself.

To his shock, she melted, as if all the tension she'd been holding inside was suddenly gone. The rigid muscles supporting her spine softened, allowing her back to curve naturally into a perfect submissive pose.

"I'm ready, Daddy."

Trust shone in her eyes, and she was so achingly beautiful...

Maybe he didn't deserve her. He was definitely too old for her, and Mitch worried he'd always remind her of what had befallen her, but he couldn't resist any longer.

Not when he wanted Zinnia so badly.

itch cupped her face and kissed her forehead. He was so gentle—it was a barely-there brush of his lips that sent a shiver down Zinnia's spine.

It was an innocent, sweet gesture—like something one might give a child—yet she couldn't begin to unpack the surfeit of emotion implicit in the press of his lips on her face.

She wanted everything he said he'd do. The spanking. The tease of his ephemeral touch.

The rope.

"Are you afraid?" he asked, pulling her from her thoughts.

"Should I be?"

He took a small step back. "I hope not, but I wouldn't be surprised if you were."

"Lots of things scare me." She closed the distance between them, wishing she could touch him. "I'm terrified of the dark. I'm afraid of people, but also of being alone. Loud noise doesn't bother me, but the quiet sometimes does—even though I came up here to get away from city sounds."

"I—"

"There's only one thing I can say with absolute certainty that I'm not afraid of, and that's you, Daddy."

"Oh, baby girl…" He traced the line of her jaw with a gentle fingertip. "You're the bravest person I've ever met. Didn't you know that?"

"After I just gave you the laundry list of things I'm afraid of?"

Mitch moved his hand to the back of her neck and squeezed gently, then leaned close and nipped her earlobe. "You were scared to try the rope swing, but you did it anyway. You drove all the way up here by yourself to work for people you don't know."

"But that was—"

He kissed her brutally, cutting off her words. The mix of feral claiming and the tenderness of his hold on her made Zinnia's knees weak and she nearly fell against him, too desperate for more to consider what she was doing.

"That was brave, baby," he whispered softly against her lips, "so fucking brave. And it was beyond ballsy for you to call out for us to find you back in Afghanistan."

Zinnia's body flushed with pleasure, erupting into goosebumps. "You were speaking English. I'd have shouted the roof down for anything that wasn't Dari."

He laughed softly, then kissed her again. It was gentler, but no less compelling. "Such bravery deserves a reward."

Mitch dropped to his knees in front of her and pushed her panties to her ankles. To her shock, he pressed his face into her center, then swirled his tongue around her clit. The surge of electric pleasure nearly stole her wits along with her breath.

"Blessed be!"

He growled something unintelligible against her pussy, then dug his fingers into her thighs, holding her still as he feasted, using the flat of his tongue to lap at her core. She'd have given almost anything to touch him, just to lay her hands on his head, but she couldn't get her arms free of the tangled fabric of her robe or the belt he'd tied loosely around her wrists.

"Delicious." Using one shoulder, he forced her thighs apart, then pushed a thick finger into her dripping channel. She moaned her approval, trying desperately to stay on her feet as Mitch rocked her world.

She'd never been one to let a partner do things to her without reciprocating but being tied... Being helpless and at his mercy unlocked something inside her. There was freedom in sexual submission. Freedom to enjoy the moment without expectation.

Freedom to... feel.

Yet *helpless* wasn't the right word. By his position kneeling at her feet, Mitch gifted her with power too. She could have stepped away at any time and trusted him to untie her if she wanted. Aside from that, she was more than capable of getting herself loose with minimal effort.

He sucked her clit into his mouth and teased the sensitive nub with the tip of his tongue as he eased a second finger inside her. Without warning, he curled them and pressed against her g-spot, then lifted his head to meet her eyes. He drew a circle around her clit with his thumb and she nearly swallowed her tongue.

"Are you going to be a good girl for Daddy?" he asked, pulling his hand away.

She'd been so close to the edge and wanted to smack Mitch upside the head for stopping. Once she managed to catch her breath enough to use actual words instead of curses, she asked, "What happens if I'm not?"

"Good girls get rewarded." Glistening with her wetness, his lips curled into a sexy grin. "Actually, so do bad girls."

The words sent a delicious tingle down her spine. It wasn't fear though. The pinch of trepidation mixed with plain, old-fashioned need was like nothing she'd ever experienced, and she wanted more.

"Then maybe I'd like to be bad."

"You have no idea how glad I am to hear that." He rose to his feet, and it almost felt like he towered over her, despite being an inch or two shorter than she was.

"Goddess." Zinnia whimpered and let her head fall to the side as his strong fingers massaged the tension from her neck. "Is this what a bad girl gets?"

"Yes. Good girls get a massage too." His soft breath tickled the short hairs on her neck and she shivered. "But good girls get to come. Bad girls have to beg for it."

MAYBE MITCH WAS TOO old for Zinnia, but he couldn't bring himself to care. Not anymore.

Not when she was here in his arms. He wanted to give her everything she'd been denied for so long. Freedom, safety…

*Love. You've been half in love with her for years.*

He brushed the thought away, knowing he couldn't tell her something like that—even if it was true. She'd run fast enough to leave a contrail, and he wasn't willing to risk chasing her away.

Gently, he turned her to face him, then tipped up her chin to make her meet his eyes. "Before we do anything, before I touch you again, you can stop at any time. All you have to do is say red. Yellow will slow everything down if it gets to be too much."

"What's wrong with saying no?"

"If I stop making you come a million times because you've said no, you might smother me in my sleep. You can choose a different safe word if you prefer."

"So, no means yes, and red means no?" Her

135

thickly lashed brown eyes sparkled with humor and she giggled. "Got it."

"And yellow means you need a break or something is bothering you."

Although her smile faded, she didn't look away. "I've been living in a perpetual state of yellow for years and I'm done. I want you to make me green. I want everything you can show me."

"Everything covers a lot of ground," he replied, repeating her words.

"Then we'll have something to do aside from fishing."

He chuckled at her tart reply, then tapped her nose. "Naughty girl."

"No, but I'd like to be."

All the blood left his brain and went straight south into his dick. Mitch would have given anything to take her into Saints and Sinners, but he'd make do with what he had.

She was already restrained with the sash from her robe. Her own sexual need would do the rest, but he'd have to go slow and be gentle. She might have had a layman's knowledge of D/s, but... Actually, he didn't know her level of experience.

"Have you played before?" he asked.

She studied him for a moment, then shook her

head. "Not the way I suspect you're thinking of. I doubt a few spanks and a little bit of anal makes me an expert, and it's been a long time."

"Did you like it?" He traced a finger down her spine, smiling at the goosebumps pebbling her silky skin. He wasn't looking for a play-by-play of her time with her past lovers, but desperately wanted to know if she'd found it enjoyable. Mitch circled her throat then bent close and nipped her ear. "Tell Daddy your secrets, baby girl."

She shuddered and let out a halting breath. "I liked both, Daddy."

"Mmm, I like hearing you call me that. Do you mind being blindfolded if I leave the lights on?"

"As long as you're with me, no. There are scarves in the top drawer of my dresser."

"There's my good girl," he murmured. Quickly, he raced to her room and retrieved a scarf, then returned and wrapped it around her eyes. "Tell me if it bothers you, okay?"

She let out a self-deprecating laugh and shook her head. "It shouldn't matter if the lights are on if I'm blindfolded."

"Can you see light through the scarf?" When she nodded, he said, "Then it matters. It's enough that you want it."

Tangled in the fabric of her robe, Zinnia's wrists were still bound behind her back. Working quickly, he freed her and let the robe drop to the floor in a puddle of silk.

"What are you doing?" she asked as he examined her slender wrists for chafing.

"Fabric isn't a good thing to use for bondage if it's going to stay there for any length of time," he murmured, holding her wrist up. "Knots can pull tight and cut off circulation. I prefer leather cuffs, but I don't have any with me."

"I have a box of a thousand condoms, so at least one of us is prepared."

He dropped her hand and moved to face her, then folded his arms over his chest. "And why, pray tell, do you have a thousand condoms?"

She pressed her lips together, but he caught the impish grin trying to curl them upward. "You know, a girl might need them."

"Hmm." He drew a finger up her ribs, noting her flinch with interest. "Tell me, baby girl, are you ticklish?"

"No, Daddy."

He scratched her side lightly, just under the curve of her breast, smirking when she let out a snorting giggle. "Are you sure?"

"P-positive." Zinnia squeaked when he dug his fingers into the skin under her arm, then burst into laughter and shied away from his touch. She snickered once more before calming herself. "They're stock for the clinic. People sometimes get embarrassed to buy them, so I keep a stash in my office."

"I should spank you for teasing me." In truth, he was delighted to see her having fun with him. To test the waters, he gave her one sharp swat across the glorious curve of her ass.

Stilling, she inhaled sharply and the skin over her cheekbones darkened almost imperceptibly into a blush. The amusement left her face as she licked her lower lip. Intensely carnal, the gesture was both innocent and tempting, and his cock hardened with desperate need.

"Mitch, I—"

"No more games, Zinnia." He untied the scarf from around her eyes and turned her to face him, then sank a hand into her damp hair. "I'm going to kiss the fuck out of you, then we're going to make love until we fall unconscious."

Once the words were out, he cursed himself. Judging by the expression of shock on her face, he'd been too forceful and revealed too much. She was rightfully gun-shy, and he wouldn't blame her a bit if she slapped him and threw him out. Hell, he didn't ask for her consent—he demanded it like he had the right.

She held his gaze for an eternity, then pressed a palm against his cheek. "I thought you'd never ask."

# CHAPTER 11

*I*t was almost like a dream. The one man who made her feel like a normal woman without three years of baggage wanted her. And the way he'd described what he planned made her realize he wanted her as badly as she wanted him.

Despite his demands, he let her initiate their kiss, touching his lips to hers so gently it almost made her cry.

"There's my good girl," he whispered against her lips.

"I thought I was supposed to be bad."

"Next time." He took control of their kiss, sweeping his tongue into her mouth to claim her as if they were already making love.

He petted her, gentling her to his touch as if he

had all the time in the world. She'd never once had a man kiss her like that—not as a prelude to sex, but like he'd have been happy to keep right on kissing her.

But she wanted more.

Swallowing a needy whimper, she broke their kiss and moved backward until her calves hit the edge of the bed. "Condoms are in that red box behind you."

"Someone is impatient." He found the box and knelt to split the tape with a thumbnail, then pulled out a handful of condoms.

"Some other someone isn't naked yet."

Chuckling, he tossed the condoms on the nightstand, then held out his arms. "Why don't you fix that, baby girl?"

Mitch made her feel powerful and beautiful. Dominance permeated every cell of his muscular body, yet he was giving her the chance to take the initiative. She wished she had half his self-confidence, but she'd get it someday.

Nothing would ever be the same, but that didn't mean she couldn't come back from her ordeal stronger and surer of herself. In fact, she'd already taken the first step by accepting a position in Vermont.

She let herself move toward him, hips loose as wetness dripped down her inner thigh. Licking her lips, she dropped to her knees at his feet and looked up at him.

A wrinkle formed between his brows, and he held out a hand. "Zinnia, I—"

"Turnabout is only fair." Without waiting for an answer, she slid his sweats down over his hips, taking several seconds to nibble the sweet ridge of his Adonis belt—just as she'd wanted to when she saw him in swim trunks.

The bulge in the front of his tight boxer briefs enticed her and she cupped him gently, relishing his indrawn gasp of pleasure as he pushed his hand into her hair. He twisted the strands around his fist yet didn't take control or try to shove her face into his groin.

It was as if he couldn't stand not touching her, and the slight stinging pull on her scalp sent a delicious shard of electric sensation into her core, making her pussy clench. She didn't even care that her hair would look like she'd stuck a finger in a light socket in the morning.

He could shave her bald for all she cared.

"Daddy's got game," she murmured, rubbing her cheek against the perfect curve of his thick shaft.

Male musk and soap filled her lungs, and she crooned her approval as she eased his boxers down to reveal a mouthwatering erection.

His hand tightened in her hair, and he tugged gently. "Daddy's going to spank your cute butt if you don't quit teasing."

She laughed and traced the sexy vein on the side of his cock with the tip of her tongue. "You say that like it's a bad thing."

It had been ages since her last time with a man, and she felt as if everything was new and somehow different. Like it meant something... more, and she wanted to worship him.

Slowly, she closed her lips around the succulent head of his cock and sucked, drawing him deeper into her mouth until he touched the back of her throat.

Too bad there was no way all of him was going to fit, but she'd have a grand time trying. Sweet precum trickled down her throat and she pulled back to swirl her tongue around the swollen glans, desperate to get every trace of the delectable fluid.

"Zinnia," he rasped, "oh, fuck!" Without warning, he hauled her to her feet, then dragged her to the bed.

Her squeak of surprise turned into a giggle as

they fell to the mattress together. Maybe his weight on top of her should have been frightening, but all she felt was warm comfort.

Mitch kissed her, then reached for a condom. "Are we still good, baby girl?"

"Good as gold." Lifting her head, she kissed his chest right over his heart.

"You're killing me, you know that?" He let out a soft groan and sat up to sheathe himself.

"But what a way to go." She grabbed his shoulders to pull him close, then wrapped her calves around his hips. "I need you now."

"Bossy." Instead of giving her what she wanted, he teased, dragging his hard cock against her center to coat himself with her moisture.

"Please!"

He thrust his hips, rubbing his cock over her clit until she thought she'd go mad. "What did you forget baby girl?"

"Mitch, please! I need you now!" She pushed a hand between their bodies and grabbed for him in a desperate attempt to get his cock where she needed it.

Instead of letting her touch him, he grabbed her wrists in one large hand and pressed them to the mattress over her head. His lips crashed against hers in another searing kiss, and he kept rubbing against her, driving her crazy with need.

"I told you bad girls have to beg."

MITCH WAS ABOUT to lose his damned mind. Zinnia was so hot, so wet.

So perfect.

She writhed under him, her legs tightening around his hips as she thrust her hips up in an attempt to get him where he wanted to be more than anything. He gritted his teeth, determined to make them both wait.

She squeezed her eyes shut and the tendons in her neck stood out in sharp relief as she strained against him. "Please, Daddy!"

A single silvery tear dripped down her cheek and she opened her eyes to meet his gaze. "Please…"

"Oh, sweetheart, that was a very good beg. I'm going to give you exactly what you want."

He kissed the tears away and slowly, giving them both time to adjust, he positioned himself at her entrance and eased his way into her clenching pussy.

Zinnia's head fell back to the pillow, and she

wriggled her hands free to clutch his shoulders. "Yes. So damned good."

Although his eyes wanted to drift closed at the sheer perfection of making love to the one woman who had captured his attention for so long, he kept his focus on her. He needed to see her face fill with passion when she came for him.

Grabbing her thigh, he pressed it down to open her to his penetration, needing every inch of her beautiful body exposed to his claiming touch.

"Please, please, please," she begged, her nails biting into his shoulders. "I—"

A tremendous crash of thunder nearly deafened him and Zinnia cried out in terror as the room went dark. A fork of lightning cracked outside, leaving the scent of ozone as rain poured down.

She bucked, barely giving him time to climb off her before she scrambled from the bed. Another shard of lightning illuminated her for a split second before leaving them in pitch darkness.

"No."

Her whisper was barely audible over the pouring rain and he cursed under his breath as he tried to creep toward her without tripping over anything. "Hey, Zinnia, I'm here. It's going to be okay. I have a flashlight and there are candles in the kitchen. Just stay still and—"

"No, no, no."

"Sweetie, I'm right here with you. We're fine."

"No!"

Her scream of rage shocked him to stillness and before he could catch her, he heard the sound of running footsteps, then a door slam.

"Shit!" He grabbed a flashlight from his duffel and chased her, praying she hadn't gone outside. "Zinnia, where are you?" he shouted.

When there was no answer, he scrambled into his sweats and went out, promising himself he'd beat her ass when he caught up to her. He spun in a circle and shouted her name again.

She didn't answer, yet a flash of lightning revealed her standing on the gravel beach of the pond, feet planted, and arms spread wide. Her hair stood out in spiral curls, wild and twisted by the wind.

He took off running toward her but skidded to a stop when she shouted at the sky.

"You cock-blocking bitch! You want a piece of me? Come on and get it!" Thunder rumbled and she let out a sharp, bitter laugh as another fork of lightning streaked through the cloud cover.

"Is that all you got? Fuck you. A year in a cave didn't break me, and you think a little rain and a light show is gonna do it?"

"Zinnia, let's get you inside, honey." He reached for her hand, but she ignored him and stepped into the water until it reached her hips.

"I'm not going to let anyone or anything make me afraid ever again," she said, her voice quieter, but still firm. "Not the dark and certainly not this lame-ass storm. Knock. It. Off."

As it had in Afghanistan the day he found her, the wind died. Thunder rumbled in the distance, but the rain softened into a gentle sprinkle instead of a downpour. A glimmer of moonlight peeked through the clouds, illuminating her in silver.

Mitch let out a breath and unclenched his hands, then scratched his head as he tried to hold back a smile. "I cannot believe you just picked a fight with a thunderstorm and won, baby."

"Hey there, Daddy." She smiled, but went deeper into the water and crooked a finger at him. "Wanna come swim with me?"

"I'm thinking we left something unfinished back in the cottage."

"We did." She swam toward him, then stood and

walked from the water. "I might like to make love to you under the stars."

"Condoms. Plus, it's still raining."

She laughed softly and kissed him, her wet hair falling over one shoulder. "Curses. Foiled by personal well-being and safety."

Mitch chuckled and ignored his thickening cock. He wasn't about to lie and say the idea didn't sound good, but he needed to get her inside and dried off before they did anything else. "And the spanking you earned for running outside naked during a thunderstorm."

Her chin went up and her expression turned mulish. "It was worth it."

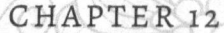

## CHAPTER 12

To Zinnia's surprise, Mitch swung her into his arms, then carried her across the gravel like a bride before setting her down on the soft grass.

"There. No walking barefoot on gravel," he murmured, wrapping an arm around her waist.

"Thanks." She cuddled closer and let out a cleansing breath as she rested her head on his shoulder. "I'm sorry if I scared you."

"It's okay. I might not understand what possessed you to yell at the weather, but it seemed to be something you needed."

She considered it for a moment, then nodded. "Yeah, I think I did."

Zinnia didn't understand her actions either. It

was as if all the anger and hurt she'd held inside for years had finally burst free. It wasn't entirely the muddled ball of terrified rage left over from her captivity either. She'd finally let go of the fear of not fitting in. Of not being perfect.

Of not being enough. It was weight she'd carried for too long that had nothing to do with Afghanistan. Mitch accepted her just the way she was—even when she let her crazy hang out.

"Do you feel better now?"

"Yes, thank you." She hummed her contentment, then asked, "Is that offer of hot chocolate still open?"

"Sure. I—"

Wearing a long raincoat and a pair of Wellington boots, Tennyson stepped in front of them, his arms crossed over his chest. "Care to tell me why you two are standing in my driveway, one of you bare-assed naked in the rain?"

Feeling her entire body flush, she stepped behind Mitch. "My fault, sir. I—"

"We went for a midnight swim," Mitch interrupted. "Since you and Chelsea enjoy it so much, we thought we'd give it a shot."

Tennyson cracked a grin, then gave them a tiny salute. "Fair enough. Carry on but try not to shout at any more thunderstorms. I don't want anything to wake Chelsea."

Whistling softly, he went back to his house and closed the door behind him.

"Goddess have mercy." Zinnia covered her face with her hands and shivered. The chill was starting to get to her. "Just the thing I wanted my new boss to see."

Mitch chuckled and took her hand to lead her back to the cottage. "Don't worry about it. You're not the first naked woman he's seen."

"I'm probably the first one he's seen throw down with the weather though." Despite her embarrassment, she felt a tiny smile trying to curl her lips. Everything was going to be okay, but she made a mental note to apologize to Tennyson the next time she saw him.

Instead of using the front door, Mitch led her around to the back of the cottage. "Let's go in through the mudroom. There are clean towels in the dryer, and you're shivering."

"That will keep us from making a mess too." She followed him inside, then wrapped the towel he offered around her hair. "Thanks."

He patted her dry with a second towel, then

smiled and shook his head. "You really do need a spanking, young lady, but you're so damned cute."

"Will you finish what we started after my spanking, Daddy?" She giggled, then took a step back. "Catch me if you can!"

He caught her around the waist before she'd taken two steps, then threw her over his shoulder. Mitch might not have been a particularly tall man, but he packed a lot of muscle on his body. He made her feel almost dainty, which was a novel thing for a woman who usually towered over other people.

Still carrying her, he detoured into the kitchen and grabbed a few emergency candles from a drawer. Although the power had come back on while they'd been outside, she appreciated the gesture.

"Shower first. You're chilled to the bone." He carried her into the bathroom, then deposited her in the tub and shucked off his sweats before joining her.

The warm water quickly eased the shivers and she let out a happy sigh as he washed her with her favorite lemon soap. "Feels good," she murmured, melting under his touch.

"I'm glad." He held up a bottle of shampoo. "Want me to wash your hair? It's already wet."

"Yes, please." She groaned as his strong fingers massaged her scalp, her need blossoming from the sensual touch of his body behind her. By the time he worked conditioner into her curls and rinsed it, she was about ready to beg him to take her on the bathroom floor. Even the gentle glide of a towel as he carefully dried her off was enough to make her shudder with desire. She tried not to think about his cock brushing against her hip every time he moved.

Using another towel, he squeezed water from her hair, then grabbed her wide-tooth comb from the vanity before leading her into the bedroom. "Have a seat on the bed so I can comb your hair."

"Oh, you don't have to. I'll just—"

His face darkened and he frowned. "Sit down, Zinnia. I might have to let you go to bed with wet hair, but you're going to let me take care of you where I can. Understand?"

Her butt hit the bed before she realized her body had moved, and another trickle of arousal seeped into her core. "Yes, Daddy."

Goddess, he was hitting all her buttons. Effortless dominance, sexy as all get-out… And he cared. Really, truly cared that she was comfortable and okay. Maybe those romance books had the right idea after all.

The bed dipped as he sat behind her and worked the comb gently through her hair. He was even careful not to tug too hard, but she was about done being coddled. It was time to get to more important matters—like easing the ache in her pussy.

She tried to gather her willpower and wait until he finished, but she was too impatient. Leaning back, she slid her hand along his muscular thigh toward his delectable cock, needing to touch it and make him just as desperate as she was. Unfortunately, he caught her hand before she could reach him.

"Naughty," he chided, putting her hand firmly in her lap. "I'm not done yet."

"I am." Although he still held a handful of her hair, she turned to face him. Before she could reach for his cock again, he grabbed her arm and tipped her over his lap.

*Whack!*

She hissed out a breath at the first stinging spank but relaxed her muscles and clutched the bedding. Warmth blossomed in her backside as he continued to spank her. It hurt, yet... No, it really didn't—especially when his cock grew hard against her side. She lowered her head and smirked, then wriggled against him.

He rumbled an unintelligible warning, then delivered several spanks to the sensitive crease where her thigh met her butt. She screeched at the sudden shock of actual pain and tried to lift herself off his lap.

"Five more," he gritted out. "These are for taking off to argue with the weather, and for teasing me when I'm trying to punish you. You're going to count them."

*Whack!*

"One, Daddy." It hurt, but she was beginning to understand his position. Tears popped and she sniffed them back before they fell. She hadn't meant to worry him. It had been a long time since she'd had anyone who cared enough to worry about her aside from family members.

*Whack!*

"Ouch! Two, Daddy."

*Whack! Whack!*

"Three, four!" Tears fell in earnest, cathartic, yet bitter too. She wasn't even sure why she was crying. Sure, it hurt, but that wouldn't have been enough to make her cry.

*Whack!*

She coughed to clear the tears from her voice. "Five, Daddy."

The words came out in a whisper, and before she could blink, he had her in his lap and wrapped tightly in his arms.

"Shh, baby girl. Your spanking is done, and everything is okay." He kissed her temple and hummed, the tune once again reminding her of wind chimes, soothing and soft.

Her backside ached and throbbed, yet it felt good too—like a reminder that even when she put herself at risk, Mitch still loved...

No. She pushed that word out of her crazy-ass head. People didn't fall in love in less than a day— not even in romance books.

HE'D HELD it together as long as he'd been able, needing to make sure she was warm and safe before he did anything else. He hadn't meant to give her an actual punishment, but seeing her out there in the open, risking a lightning strike...

Mitch petted her back, gentling her down from her spanking. "That's my good girl," he crooned softly as her tears slowed, then stopped.

"Thank you," she murmured. "My mama would call that a come to Jesus moment."

He chuckled softly, then tipped up her chin to make her look at him. "What would you call it?"

"A long overdue showdown with nature and Gaia. I'm Pagan." Leaning close, she kissed him. "I'm sorry I scared you. That wasn't my intent."

Still smiling, he shook his head. "Normally, when a baby girl earns herself a punishment, her Daddy asks her to apologize and thank him. You stole my thunder right along with the storm's."

Her eyes sparkled with humor. "My butt is a little tender. Can we hold off on the punishment for that?"

"Oh, sweetheart, that deserves a reward."

Mitch kissed her, tracing her plump lower lip with the tip of his tongue. She tasted like warm sugar and lemon, sweet and heady, and unwilling to rush things, he pulled away.

"Mmm. Nice reward." She licked her lips and leaned closer for another kiss.

"That was my reward." Forcing himself to pull away, he helped her lie back on the bed and carefully spread her hair out over her head to allow it to dry. "Now it's time for yours."

Without being asked, she stretched her arms above her head and laced her fingers together. "Can't wait."

"Such a good girl." He kissed a path down her sternum, then took a pert nipple into his mouth. When he swirled his tongue around the delicious bud, her hands fell to his head, holding him against her. He gave it one last suck, then let it pop free.

"Hands above your head, or I stop."

"Yes, Daddy." A faint smile blossomed on her face, and she put her hands where they belonged. "I'll be good."

"I see those fingers crossing, young lady." Despite his words, he returned her smile, then sucked her nipple into his mouth again, relishing her throaty moan of pleasure.

He wanted to see if he could make her come just from nipple stimulation, but there was no way he'd be able to wait. His cock throbbed almost painfully, and judging by the way her hips bucked, she was just as desperate as he was.

Trailing kisses across her stomach, he moved down her body and used his shoulders to part her thighs. Her neatly trimmed hair glistened with moisture, beckoning him closer. The scent of her arousal surrounded him in a cloud of sensual heat, and he lowered his mouth to her core, needing a small taste before he did anything else.

"Please, Daddy." She whined the words softly as

he sucked her clit into his mouth, but he didn't need to hear her beg.

He gave her pussy one last swipe with his tongue and lifted his head. "Shh. Are you ready for me?"

She bucked against him and reached for a condom, then held it out. "More than."

He reached for it, but she caught his hand and brought it to her lips. "Very, very ready, Daddy. Make with the protection and fuck me, please."

"So demanding, yet polite too." He took the condom and nipped her ear, then licked it to soothe the sting. As much as he wanted to keep teasing her, he just... couldn't.

Quickly, he slid the condom over his erection, then rolled them over until she was on top, her knees next to his hips. When she blinked at him in surprise, he cupped her cheek, running a thumb over her cheekbone. "Make yourself feel good, baby."

Her only response was a low moan as she positioned him at her entrance and sank down, taking him deep.

"That's it." He pushed his hips up to meet her but resisted the urge to hold her still for his possession. Yet he nearly lost all control when she swiveled her hips and rocked slowly, driving him insane with need. If she wasn't careful, he'd be the one begging.

"Yes…" She hissed the word and rested her hands on his chest.

"Sit up and play with those gorgeous breasts," he ordered. "Use one hand and put the other on your pussy. I want to see what makes you feel good."

"You make me feel good."

"I'm glad." He held her hips, more to help her with her balance than to control her, but he couldn't resist the urge to thrust up into her welcoming channel.

She tightened around him, her inner walls fluttering as her climax built. He didn't look at her hands though. All his attention was focused on her beautiful face.

Her mouth was open, almost slack with pleasure, and there was a tiny wrinkle between her brows. Her hips jerked and she moved faster, riding him as she chased the threads of passion.

"Come for me, baby. Let me see you explode."

"I…" Her head fell back as her pussy clamped down on his shaft. She stilled and screamed shrilly. "Mitch!"

Watching her come was the most incredibly intimate thing he'd ever experienced. He'd seen a look of utter bliss on people before, but none of them were Zinnia.

## CHAPTER 13

She collapsed against Mitch's chest, barely able to catch her breath after the most stupendous orgasm she'd ever experienced. Her vision even went fuzzy and dark around the edges as aftershocks pulsed through her body.

"There's my good girl," Mitch whispered, brushing his lips over the shell of her ear. Without waiting for her to answer, he pushed his hand between their bodies and pressed his thumb over her clit, rubbing the overstimulated flesh. "Come for me again."

"No... Mitch, I can't. Please!" She tried to wriggle free, but he banded an arm around her waist to hold her still.

"Yes, you can."

She shuddered as another dark wave of pleasure gathered strength in her core. Despite being in a position of supposed control, she was helpless to resist his will as he thrust into her. His teeth were bared, throwing the angles of his face into sharp relief. The sheer weight of his focus was almost frightening, but he made her feel *seen*—like she was the only thing in his world.

"Goddess!" The wave crested over as he slammed into her one last time, his fingers digging into her hip almost painfully. He pinched her clit hard and her body seized as unspeakable pleasure dragged her under.

He let out a tearing groan and swelled inside her, pulling her tightly against him as he panted in her ear. His body flexed into rigidity, then relaxed, but he didn't let her go.

Not that she wanted him to. Being in his arms was perfect.

"God, Zinnia." His raspy sex voice tickled her senses, making her wonder if either of them were up for round two.

Lifting her head, she smiled, but was caught in his compelling light brown eyes. He looked at her like he had no plans to ever let her go, and she wasn't sure what to do about it.

She couldn't let herself get attached. He'd be leaving soon, and... No, she was getting too far ahead of herself. They'd had great sex. Amazing sex. She liked him. None of that meant either one of them would want a future together. Instead of panicking or letting her mind spin back into anxiety, she tried to let it go and enjoy the moment.

"I know," she finally said. Her voice was hoarse with exertion, and she cleared her throat. "That was... yeah."

She tried to wriggle free, sure she was crushing him. Instead of letting her go, he rolled until she was nestled on her side against his chest.

"Do you want the lights on?"

The dark had lost its frightening grip on her and she didn't need it anymore. "No, Daddy."

"Okay." He fumbled around and switched off the bedside lamp, then wrapped his arm around her once more. "Go to sleep, baby girl. I'll be right here with you."

"Sounds like an excellent plan."

Zinnia fell asleep to the scent and sound of gentle rain, knowing she was completely safe.

"Hey, baby girl. Time to wake up."

She opened her eyes and blinked. Mitch was already up and wearing shorts and a T-shirt. He set a tray laden with coffee and food on the nightstand.

"Wow." She sat up and tucked the sheet under her arms, then crossed her legs into a lotus position. "Thank you."

"No problem. I was pretty sure scrambled eggs, toast, and sausage wouldn't be triggering for you, so I had Tennyson bring over a few things to tide you over until Kaden gets back with your grocery order."

"Oh, but—"

"You had coffee and milk," he interrupted, handing her a plate. "I'm sure you're not about to tell me that's all you planned to have for breakfast."

"No, Daddy." She tried to swallow a giggle but wasn't entirely successful. "I did actually plan to run to the store this morning though."

"Since it's already taken care of, eat up and we'll go fishing."

"Sounds like fun." She ate a bite of fluffy eggs and moaned. It might have had something to do with toe-curling sex followed by a good night's sleep, but it seemed her appetite had come back with a vengeance. "This is really good. Thanks again."

"My pleasure." He sat next to her and ate his meal, then smiled and gave her the last sausage from his plate. He gathered their dishes, then said, "Get dressed while I clean up and get out the fishing gear."

"What do we use for bait? Do we need to find worms?" The thought didn't appeal, but she wasn't about to turn down a new experience over something as silly as touching a worm.

"No, we'll be using flies."

"I think I'd rather dig up worms."

He laughed, nearly spilling the tray of dirty dishes. "No, baby. Flies are artificial lures made to look like insects."

"Huh. I had no idea."

"People use all kinds of bait for fishing, but trout like bugs." He carried the tray to the door, then added, "Meet me in the kitchen when you're ready."

"What should I wear?"

"Shorts and a T-shirt. I can loan you a ball cap if you don't have a hat. It's going to be a scorcher today."

Ten minutes later, she was dressed in a pair of cutoff jeans, a vivid blue halter top, and a floppy straw hat. She didn't bother with a lick of makeup, and left her hair in a mass of loose curls. There wasn't much point in fussing with it when she planned to swim after her fishing date.

She snickered, tickled at the idea of fishing as a first date. With a man she'd already slept with.

"What's so funny?" Mitch asked. His hands were laden with a tackle box and two fishing rods.

"I was just thinking I've never had such an interesting first date."

"We can do something else if you prefer."

"I really want to catch a fish and have it for lunch." After dropping her phone on the charger, she eased the box from his fingers and walked outside into a glorious midsummer morning.

HE SET up a couple of chairs on the fishing dock, then showed her how to attach a lure to her line. It didn't seem possible, but Zinnia was even more gorgeous fresh out of bed. It wasn't even her physical appearance though. The lines of tension were gone from her face and her shoulders were relaxed.

She looked... happy.

"Okay, I'll show you how to cast. You're going to aim for the shady spot under that tree. Ready?"

"Can I watch you first?"

"Sure." Making sure she could see, he cast into

the spot he'd indicated, then reeled in a bit of line. "Do you want me to do it again?"

"Probably, but I'm going to try it first. Then you can tell me how to fix it when I mess up."

He chuckled and handed her a pole. "The good thing about fishing is that even a bad cast has a chance to catch a fish. When I was a kid, one of my friends caught a flounder through a hole in a pier with a piece of bologna tied to a string."

Giggling, Zinnia walked to the edge of the dock and did a remarkably good job duplicating his cast. When her lure landed just a few feet from his, she squealed and clapped a hand over her mouth.

"Sorry, I forgot we're supposed to be quiet for fishing."

Mitch hugged her from behind and kissed her bare shoulder. "Well, it's probably not a great idea to use the swing while someone is fishing, but we can talk. Or nap in the sunshine if you prefer."

"Sounds like my idea of a pastime." She put her rod in the holder next to her chair and sat, her long legs stretched out in front of her, then gazed pensively over the pond and lapsed into silence.

Although he wondered if she was working through some problem in her head, he decided not to disturb her. He'd come here for peace himself, and she needed it more than he ever had.

"I'm sorry," she suddenly said, breaking the silence.

"For what?" He twitched his line in hopes of attracting a hungry fish.

"For last night. I hate that I kind of insisted on intimacy after you said you weren't interested. And then I had the mother of all meltdowns, which couldn't have been fun for you."

"Oh, I'm very interested." He reached across the space separating them and took her hand. "I'm just worried I'm too old for you."

"I forgot you're two steps away from a nursing home," she muttered under her breath.

He stilled and didn't dare look at her. The words and even the vocal inflection sounded so much like Serena it was as if she was sitting in Zinnia's chair.

"What did you say?" He faced her, knowing it was absurd to expect a woman who had been dead almost a year to be speaking.

"You're two steps away from a nursing home," she repeated. "It doesn't bother me. Maybe it would be different if I was younger, but..." She shrugged, then cracked a smile. "You're in amazing physical shape, and I'd be willing to bet you take care of yourself. Aside from that, you sure don't make love like a man in a nursing home."

"Thanks, I think?" He couldn't help a small smile at Zinnia's sass.

"No charge." She leaned back and closed her eyes, then sighed. "But it's also made me realize I've been a judgmental cow about something. My parents split up when I was gone, and my father married a woman about five years older than I am. The gap between them is about the same as it is for you and me, and I was pretty awful to them."

"Ouch."

"You can say that again." She walked to the edge of the dock and looked out over the water. "I guess I had this image in my head of everything being exactly the same as I left it, and now I have a half-sibling on the way."

He went to her and wrapped his arms loosely around her waist. She leaned back against him and rested her head on his shoulder. "What's even worse is that I know I'm being ridiculous about it."

"Do you think about moving back?"

She turned in his arms and kissed him, letting her tongue slide past his lips as she pulled him close. A sudden splash broke them apart, and her rod bent almost double as they watched.

"You caught a fish, baby girl!"

"Blessed be! What do I do now?"

Her giggles as he helped her land her fish were infectious, and he laughed outright as he swept her catch into a net. "It's a big one too! Definitely enough to feed us both lunch."

"Hello, lunch," she crooned, reaching through the net to touch silvery scales. Her brows drew together, and she looked up at him. "Will Tennyson mind?"

"No. He just asks that we release them if they won't be eaten and to make sure we don't leave a mess when we clean them."

"Clean them?"

"You'll see." He put the trout on a stringer, then gave it to her to carry it back to the cottage while he took care of their gear.

Zinnia held his hand as they walked home, and he had a hard time imagining anything more perfect. Mitch just wished she'd answered his question about leaving Vermont.

# CHAPTER 14

Fishing was fun. Catching a fish was beyond exciting. Scaling and cleaning a fish was...

She swallowed and held her breath as Mitch showed her how to open up her future lunch and scoop out the insides. Maybe she'd feel better after washing the scales off her arms and legs. Who knew one fish would create such a mess?

"I think I understand why Tennyson wants us to clean up after this. I bet it attracts critters."

"Exactly. Now, watch. I'm going to show you how filet it, then I want you to try."

"What happens to all the insides? We can't just dump it in the trash. It'll start to smell." To her surprise, she was able to cut a filet almost as nice as the one he'd done, despite her hands being slippery with things she didn't want to think about.

"We usually carry it to the other side of the pond and let nature take its course." He folded the filets in a large piece of white butcher paper and dumped the waste into a bucket. "We'll put these in the fridge for later."

"Good idea. I'm not remotely hungry." They held hands as they walked around the pond to dispose of the fish waste. The day was warming and the water looked so inviting…

Then again, she and Mitch would be getting naked to clean up. She smirked and wiped a fish scale off his chin. "I'm sure we can think of something to do until supper."

"You, Ms. Turner, are a tease." He swatted her butt. "We need to change into jeans and boots. I have a surprise for you."

"Oh? What is it?"

His eyes crinkled into a smile and he winked, making her knees go almost rubbery. "It wouldn't be a surprise if I told you, but it's something I hope you like."

Twenty minutes later, they were on the road to an unknown destination. Mitch still wouldn't tell her where they were going, but she was having a wonderful time just watching the scenery. The trees eventually gave way to tidy farms surrounded by stone walls, with clapboard houses that wouldn't have looked out of place in a film about the American Revolution.

"Would you be comfortable if I asked you to close your eyes?" Mitch asked, slowing his car.

Obediently, she laid her hands over her eyes. "Okay, Daddy. I'm ready."

"Such a good girl." He slowed even further and turned, then drove for a bit longer before parking. "I'll help you out, and in just a few minutes, you can see your surprise."

Even a week ago, she wouldn't have been able to do what he was asking. Surprises were a bugbear for her, and she'd hated them. Until Mitch, nothing good ever came from any unexpected event. Yet with him, everything was different.

She was different.

He held her close as he walked her across pea gravel, and she smelled the familiar and welcome scent of horses. It had been years since she'd last ridden but had gotten pretty good before her mother decided she'd had enough of that particular skill.

She heard the soft sound of a horse mouthing a

bit, and a slight scuffle of hooves on gravel, letting her know her guess had been accurate.

Unwilling to spoil his fun, Zinnia kept her mouth shut until he said, "Okay, baby girl. You can look now."

She lowered her hands and blinked to let her vision adjust to the bright sunlight, then looked up. And up some more at the biggest horse she'd ever seen. "Holy crap, you're a monster!"

Jennifer laughed as she walked around from the animal's other side. "Well, his name is Sully, but I promise he's a sweetheart."

"He's a Clydesdale crossed with a school bus, right?" She laid a hand on his nose when he tried to nuzzle her shoulder. "And where the heck did you find a saddle to fit him? Come to think of it, how did you manage to get it on him in the first place? There's no way you could reach."

Wherever the tack had come from, it was expensive and well-fitted. Despite being supersized, the dressage saddle wouldn't have looked out of place in a show barn and the double reins were exactly the kind she used to prefer.

Jennifer giggled and pointed at a large mounting stage. She'd obviously stood on it to saddle him. "He's a Shire. His previous owner passed away and he's looking for a new home. The tack is all custom and goes with him."

Letting out a puff of air, Sully rested his chin on Zinnia's shoulder, looking for all the world like he was about to fall asleep. "Oh, well, I—"

"A little birdie told me you ride." After glancing at Mitch, Jennifer handed her a dressage whip and a helmet, then added, "He's schooling third level, but isn't much for jumping... obviously. And aside from Tennyson, you're about the only one tall enough to not look dorky riding him."

"Blessed be, Mitch! How far back did you stalk my social media?" She'd quit riding when she was seventeen or so, meaning he'd had to have gone through over a decade of photos.

"Probably not much past when you got your braces off." He gave her an unrepentant grin. "Go on. You know you want to."

Goddess, she really did. "It's been a while, so let's see if I remember how."

ZINNIA CANTERED AROUND THE ARENA, looking so happy it made his chest hurt. He wouldn't know a good rider from a bad one, but she was clearly in no danger of falling off and he was willing to believe Jennifer's murmurs of approval.

"I don't think she'll adopt him," he finally said. It was a huge responsibility, and she was still getting used to not being a captive. She was also very hesitant about new things, although he hoped he was helping her with that.

"Oh, ye of little faith." She leaned against the fence and waved as Zinnia made another lap. "I have the gift of matching each of my rescues with just the right home. Zinnia might not take Sully today, but he's definitely found a new person to own."

"Isn't that supposed to be the other way around?"

"Nope. Animals choose their people, ergo, they are the owners."

Zinnia chirped at the horse and must have given him some signal Mitch couldn't see. Instead of cantering, he slowed, and his front legs moved as if he was skipping.

"Oh, dang. She's really good!" Jennifer said.

"I'll take your word for it."

Another imperceptible signal brought the animal to a slow trot, then a walk. She dropped the reins, letting him stretch his neck down as they took another few turns around the arena.

"How much is his adoption fee and is there a

boarding barn close?" she asked as she came to a stop in front of them.

"You can keep him here, and there's no fee," Jennifer replied. "Board is three hundred a month, mostly because he's a hay disposal unit and you'll be funding my indoor arena project."

"Um… wow. Okay, thanks!" She hopped down and loosened Sully's saddle. "I'll be another hour or so, Mitch. Then we can have that fish for supper."

"Kaden will be back with your groceries by then, so you'll have something to go with it," Jennifer replied. "Grooming supplies are in the bin near the wash bay. Want some help?"

Zinnia smiled and touched her forehead to the white blaze on Sully's face. "No, I'm good."

As she led her new horse away, Jennifer leaned over and whispered, "Told ya so."

"Brat."

Zinnia fell asleep on the drive home, but he didn't mind. She hadn't gotten enough rest the night before, and they'd had a busy day. By her own admission, her physical condition wasn't as good as it should have been, but maybe having Sully would encourage her to work on her fitness.

If not… He had a crop of his own that might do the trick.

He understood her reticence though. She'd been isolated for too long, and going into a crowded gym must have been overwhelming. Yet for the first time, he could envision himself being there for her. Not just for a few days until he moved on, but forever.

After parking next to her SUV, he touched her gently, then said, "Hey, baby girl, we're home."

She jumped, bumping her head on the roof of his car, then scowled upward. "Sorry," she said, rubbing her head.

"You okay?"

"Yeah, just being an idiot."

"No, I shouldn't have touched you like that. I'm sorry I scared you."

Her lips curved into a smile, and she leaned over to kiss his cheek. "Mitch, I may never get over being jumpy, but with you, it's okay. I'm okay. I—"

The blare of a horn shattered their moment, and she turned to see who had interrupted them. A black limousine appeared, moving slowly up the driveway.

"Must be one of Tennyson's friends."

"Or not," Mitch replied when the vehicle continued toward the cottage. "Were you expecting someone?"

"No. I don't know anyone here aside from you

and everyone I met yesterday. The windows are too dark. I can't see…"

Her voice trailed off and she gasped as the driver parked and got out to open the passenger door. A woman wearing a white pantsuit stepped out, wrinkling her nose at the gravel under her high-heeled sandals. Aside from silver hair cut into a chin-length bob, she looked just like Zinnia, making him realize the woman was her mother or other close relative.

"Oh, no. No, no, no." Zinnia hugged herself and squeezed her eyes shut.

"Who is that?"

"Goddess, please, no." Instead of answering, she got out of his car and straightened her spine in a remarkable imitation of the woman striding toward her.

The woman stopped and gave her a derisive glance. "Zinnia, dear. What on earth happened to your hair? And what are you wearing?"

Her southern drawl was somehow clipped and biting, and he gritted his teeth. *Bless your heart* was going to come out of her mouth; he was sure of it.

Zinnia was gorgeous, and it had nothing to do with what she wore or anything else. She was beautiful to him because he…

He swallowed the word, knowing he couldn't

admit it even to himself. Focusing, he pulled Zinnia into his arms and squeezed gently. "Baby, who is that?"

She swallowed hard and pasted a smile on her face, then wriggled free of his embrace. It physically hurt to let her walk away from him.

"I wasn't expecting you to visit." Zinnia stopped in front of the woman and accepted an air kiss.

"That's probably because you've been ignoring my calls." She sniffed as she glanced at Mitch. "At least you've hired a… whatever he is, but you know better than to get familiar with the help."

If that was Zinnia's mother, Mitch had no idea how she'd managed to grow up to be so kind after being raised with someone so rude, but kept his mouth shut, waiting for Zinnia to correct her. He didn't want to be the cause of an argument, yet he wasn't going to allow himself to be insulted again.

"This is Mitch Sakurai, the man who rescued me in Afghanistan. Mitch, this is… my mother."

"Jeanette Tatum Turner. It's a pleasure, I'm sure." She glanced at his outstretched hand but didn't offer hers. "You have my most heartfelt thanks for bringing my baby home, but if you'll excuse us, Zinnia and I have to discuss when she's coming home to her family. We've been worried sick."

Without another word, she grasped Zinnia's elbow in a manicured hand and led her into the cottage, leaving him standing in the driveway. When the door shut behind them, he grunted irritably and got into his car.

He didn't know why he expected Zinnia to defend him. He was nothing to her. Zinnia's mother might have been an insufferable snob, but she was family. It was no wonder she hadn't answered his question about moving back to St. Louis.

That didn't make sense though. Why would she take a job or adopt one of Jennifer's horses if she planned to turn around and go home?

Setting his jaw, he got on the road. It wasn't any of his business, and she had to do what was best for her. He'd drive around for an hour or two, then return to pack up his stuff after she and her mother had time to chat.

It was time to get on with his life.

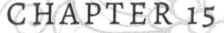

## CHAPTER 15

he door shut firmly, making Zinnia jump. She heard the sound of a car starting and dashed to the window, her heart skipping a beat when she watched Mitch drive away.

"So, this is where you're living?" Jeanette asked. "It's... rustic."

"No," Zinnia whispered, her hands tightening on the windowsill. Fear, choking and thick, made her vision waver. He was going away, and not even memories of her cave terrified her as much as the thought of Mitch leaving her.

"Then where are you living? The larger house isn't much better than this one, although I suppose it has a certain charm."

Before she could escape to chase him down, his

car vanished behind the row of trees lining the driveway. Tears welled, but she brushed them away before turning to face Jeanette. Zinnia knew better than to show emotion during a confrontation with her. "I like it, and I found a very good job."

If she could manage to convince her mother to return to St. Louis, maybe Mitch would come back. She didn't blame him a bit for leaving, but wished he'd given her a chance to explain.

"No decent restaurants, no country club, no valet parking…" She arched an eyebrow at Zinnia then swiped a fingertip over a lampshade. "No maid service. I can't imagine you'll be happy here."

"You're kidding, right?" Zinnia arched a brow and walked into the kitchen, then opened the fridge. To her surprise, it was stocked full of groceries. Not only had Kaden shopped for her, but he'd put everything away.

And her mother thought she'd even consider leaving?

Most importantly, there was still most of a bottle of wine in the fridge, and alcohol was usually the best way of coping with Jeanette. "I've managed to live without those things for years. At least I have a bed, a kitchen, and a bathroom here."

Jeanette followed her into the kitchen and

clucked her tongue. "Well, there's no reason for you to live that way now, is there? When are you coming home?"

She opened the first cupboard she came to and pulled out a plastic tumbler with a cartoon character on it, then filled it to the brim with wine. After taking a long drink, she said, "I'm not. I'm staying here."

"Nonsense." Jeanette opened her tiny Gucci clutch and pulled out a slim phone. "I know a lovely man who is very interested in meeting you. I've scheduled us for a spa day, which you obviously need, then we'll meet him for supper at the club."

"Mama, I—"

"He's an orthodontist, so I'm sure you'll have something in common."

"Not unless newborns have teeth," Zinnia muttered, but her mother wasn't listening.

"You don't have a maid, so I suppose I'll help you pack. I have a jet on standby waiting to take us home. We can hire someone to drive your car back or just sell it and buy another."

She drained the last of the wine and set the cup on the counter. "I'm not going back to St. Louis."

"Zinnia, be reasonable. You can't expect me to believe—"

"I said, I'm not going back to St. Louis!" she shouted. "You're not listening. You never listen, so I'm not sure why I'm at all surprised."

Jeanette blinked, and her lips parted in surprise. Her face darkened with a scowl and she crossed her arms. "Well! That's rude!"

"As rude as you referring to the man who saved my life as the help? That rude?"

"If you had introduced me properly, I'd have been more gracious."

"I told you who he was, but I forgot you think the only people who deserve manners are those with money. How silly of me." Jeanette opened her mouth, but Zinnia spoke right over her. "The thing is, I'm pretty sure I'm falling in love with him. I will also be more than grateful if I can live in Vermont for the rest of my life."

"You can't mean that. What about everything you're leaving behind?" Jeanette wrung her hands, for once looking legitimately upset. "The culture, decent food, your family. You can't pretend you don't want those things. What will you do here?"

"Did you know I've never toasted a marshmallow over an open fire before? I got to do that last night, and swing on a rope into the water. Today, Mitch helped me catch my first fish. I also adopted a horse.

Do you remember how much I loved riding? But you made me quit."

"Well, you had gymnastics, piano, and voice lessons, and—"

"There's a piano right in there," Zinnia replied, pointing toward the living room. "I was always too tall for gymnastics, and no matter how much you spent on voice lessons, I still can't carry a tune. The point is, they were things *you* thought I should be doing, and you made me quit the things *I* loved."

Jeanette studied her for a moment, a pensive expression on her face. "You never said a word, and you were always so cheerful. I just assumed you were fine with my decisions."

"I didn't think you'd listen." She poured more wine into her cup and looked out over the pond. "Do you remember when I begged you to let me stay on the hockey team? I was good at it. Do you remember how happy I was at practices, and that I used to have a signed Wayne Gretzky trading card before…"

She swallowed the rest of the sentence. It was gone like the rest of her childhood mementoes, discarded when she was assumed to be dead.

"You were ten, and there were all those rough boys. It wasn't appropriate."

"Because of the boys or because it wasn't a country club-approved sport? The same thing happened with swimming when I was five, but you blamed that on not wanting to deal with my hair."

Unsurprisingly, Jeanette didn't answer.

Turning to face her, Zinnia leaned against the counter and crossed her ankles. "Goddess help me, I tried but I can't fit myself into your mold anymore. I want to swim in the pond and catch trout for lunch, and not give a single thought to whether I look good enough for supper at the club. I'm praying it freezes over in the winter so I can skate again. I want to ride my horse every day without caring about my lip liner. I want a night sky without light pollution, and crickets and bullfrogs singing me to sleep. I want maple syrup frozen in snow and nature and growing things around me instead of a river valley pasta bowl of interstates and crazy traffic every time I go out."

"You could live in Chesterfield and have those things."

She sighed and pinched the skin between her brows. "If I live in Chesterfield, I won't have Mitch. It won't be okay that I can't eat rice. It won't be okay that I'm afraid of the dark, and of crowds, or how I'm walking on eggshells every minute of every day in case I have a trigger or a meltdown or…"

*Pick a fight with a thunderstorm.*

Zinnia closed her eyes, then shook her head. "I told you why I can't eat rice, but everyone insisted I'd be fine with Aunt Jessica's dirty rice because it wasn't plain. Then y'all had the nerve to be shocked and insulted when I gagged on it."

Before Jeanette could answer, Zinnia held up a hand. She was going to say all the things she'd been holding back for months and wasn't about to let anyone stop her.

"Instead of asking me if I was off my meds, Mitch suggested I make it with couscous. It sounds weird and I can't imagine what it would taste like, but he made it okay to not be okay." She hauled in a breath and swallowed. "I'm not going to let you take away something I love ever again."

"You don't fall in love because of hero worship, Zinnia. He's also shorter than you."

That wasn't the reason she loved him, and their relative heights had nothing to do with it. She didn't want to get into it with her mother, but watching him walk away made her realize she didn't want to live without him. "Everyone is shorter than me. Besides, when have I ever cared about that?"

A surprising glint of humor sparkled in Jeanette's eyes. "The orthodontist isn't. You could wear a three-inch heel and he'd still be taller."

"Blessed be! Did you measure the poor man?"

"Well, not personally, but it was a definite plus in his favor." Jeanette blew out a breath between pursed lips and lowered her head. "I... I'm sorry, baby. I didn't know we'd made it so hard on you."

Zinnia nodded, accepting the apology. "This is my home now. I'm not okay yet, but I think here with Mitch... maybe someday I could be."

Something outside caught Jeanette's attention, but she turned to give Zinnia a smile. "Do you really love him?"

"Yes, but I don't know if he loves me back."

"Okay. Got more of that wine for your mama? And don't bother looking for a wineglass."

*Okay?* That was all Jeanette had to say? Silently, Zinnia fumed and poured the last of the bottle into another cartoon tumbler and sat next to her at the breakfast bar. This was the most open and honest conversation she'd ever had with her mother, and it didn't make her feel like she was about to be sick.

"When you came home to us, I was desperate to make everything perfect for you. I had my baby girl back, but you weren't the same smiling young woman who went off on her adventures. You did everything by yourself and refused to accept my help. You refused to talk to your father, and even your sisters couldn't reach you. I... I guess I was hurt."

"Sorry, Mama. I didn't mean to—"

"I can't even imagine what it was like for you, and I know you don't like to talk about it, but I think you're one of the strongest people I've ever met," Jeanette finally said after taking a sip of her wine. "I hope you find what you're looking for up here, but always know that you can come home whenever you want."

The words, forever longed for, almost shocked her speechless and she blinked back tears. "Thank you, Mama."

"I should have said it weeks ago. Anyway, I'm going to finish my wine and head out so you can go chase down your man. Will you give him my apologies for being rude?"

"Yes, I'm sure he'll appreciate it."

"I'm going to stay in Colchester for another day or two if you want to bring Mitch to meet me properly."

"I'll ask him."

"Thank you. Tell him he's welcome to come visit

with you too." Leaning over, she kissed Zinnia's cheek, then added, "And happy belated birthday, sweetheart. I'm going to miss you."

*ARE you really going to leave her in another cave?*

Mitch slammed on the brakes before he reached the road leading away from Tennyson's property, then turned around.

He had no idea what he'd been thinking. She wasn't like her mother. If they hadn't looked so much alike, he'd have bet they weren't even related. Maybe there was a small bit of pampered princess in Zinnia though. He smiled at the memory of her in that orange dress and heels, but she was just as beautiful—just as *Zinnia*—covered in fish scales and wearing shorts.

Yet he didn't want to disturb them either. He wanted to give Zinnia a chance to stand up for herself. Keeping his footsteps silent, he crept to the kitchen window. Eavesdropping on a private conversation was never a good idea, but he couldn't stop himself, or the surge of anger at what her mother had done to her.

Yet... His baby girl was doing it! She was taking back the right to live her own life. And...

She loved him.

He took a step back, inadvertently kicking a few pebbles. Every cell in his body demanded that he go to her, but he forced himself to wait and let her finish her confrontation with her mother. Maybe she'd appreciate the rescue, but she needed to know she could stand on her own.

Mitch just wanted to be there when she stumbled. He kept listening, making mental notes on everything Zinnia wanted. Simple things, like listening to crickets and bullfrogs as she fell asleep, but experiences denied to her, first by her family, then by her captivity.

She'd have them all.

Thankfully, Zinnia and her mother soon came to a détente. He wasn't sure how much longer he could have stood out there listening. He wanted her in his arms, wanted to soothe those old hurts. Wanted to promise her he'd never try to take away the things she loved.

Quietly, he let himself into the cottage, then strode into the kitchen. Before he could say anything, Zinnia rushed into his arms, the force of her hug knocking him back a step.

She peppered his face with kisses, and squeezed him hard. "I thought I was going to have to chase you."

"I couldn't let my baby girl go." He inhaled the sweet scent of her hair, then cupped her face. "I will always be there to bring you into the sunshine."

She burst into tears, her shoulders quaking as she dug her fingers into his back. "You c-came for me. I knew you would."

"I'm sorry I didn't stay with you," he said, brushing tears off her cheeks. "I shouldn't have left you."

Zinnia sniffed, then grabbed a paper towel to clean up her face. "I—"

"Mr. Sakurai," Jeanette interrupted. "Before I leave, I want to apologize for being rude. My daughter rightly called me on it, so I'd like to start over if I may."

"Of course." It didn't take much effort to let go of his irritation. Jeanette was obviously trying, and considering she was Zinnia's mother, he'd make the effort to get along with her. "Colonel Mitchell Sakurai, United States Army, retired."

She clasped his hand and gave him a wry smile. "Jeanette Tatum Turner, former trophy wife, current day trader and philanthropist, and..." She glanced at

Zinnia, then added, "Somewhat insensitive mother, but I'm going to do better."

"It's a pleasure to meet you."

"You as well. And you have our most profound thanks for bringing Zinnia home to us." She tugged him close and kissed his cheek, surprising him. "Even if you're keeping her up here in the middle of nowhere."

"You're very welcome." He stepped back and wrapped an arm around Zinnia. "She's a treasure."

"You're right about that." Jeanette gathered her purse, then said, "I'll be going now, but let's meet for supper tomorrow."

"Sure. We can split the distance and meet in St. Albans."

"All right." She hugged them both, squeezing tightly, then stepped back. "I'll see you soon."

When the door shut behind her, Mitch hid a sigh of relief and smiled at Zinnia. "With luck, your first meeting with my parents will be a bit easier."

Lips bowing into a smile, she giggled, then rested her head on his shoulder. "If I can finally stand up to Jeanette Tatum Turner, I can handle anything."

"I know you can, baby girl." Mitch tipped up her chin, then kissed her, relishing her little whine of pleasure. Breaking their kiss, he asked, "So, which of the things on your bucket list do you want to do first?"

"What? I don't understand."

"Well, you already rode your horse, fished, swam, and listened to crickets as you fell asleep. The skating and maple popsicles will have to wait until winter though."

Her cheeks darkened and she smacked his shoulder gently. "You overheard all that?"

"Yep."

She wriggled free and faced the window. "What else did you hear?"

He touched her arm and turned her around. "The important thing is what you need to hear. I love you, Zinnia. I think I have since I first heard about you and stalked your social media even though everyone thought you were dead."

When her lip quivered, he thought she might cry again, but a glorious smile blossomed on her face and she leapt into his arms. "Thank the goddess. I love you too, Daddy. So, so much."

"Me too, baby girl." Cupping her head, he touched his lips to hers, but let her take control of the kiss.

"I think I want to add something to my bucket list, Daddy."

"What's that?"

"I still want to make love to you under the stars."

Mitch feathered a touch along her collarbone and her eyes dilated with need. "We'll have to wait until after dark, but I think that can be arranged."

"The sun is technically a star."

"Mmm. You're right. What are we waiting for?"

"Seems to me you're waiting for an invitation," she countered. "Maybe I should have it printed and engraved?"

"So naughty."

"What are you going to do about it?"

"Hmm." He unbuckled his belt and slid it from the loops. "Seems I need to teach a baby girl to mind her manners."

"Eeep!"

She darted out the kitchen door, her giggling squeals filling the air with the sound of her joy. Tossing his belt aside, Mitch gave chase.

He'd never let her go again. No matter what.

# EPILOGUE

Scowling, Serena tried to ignore Edith's cackling laughter.

"Let me get this straight," Edith said, after catching her breath. "You got yourself into a bargain with Lucifer, then you managed to be dumb enough to get caught by a baby witch."

"Shut up, Edith," Serena muttered. "I'm not listening to you."

Pink wings folded behind her, Edith perched on her husband Dimitri's lap. She chuckled and wiped her eyes as her other husband Paul stroked her shoulders. "Honey, you are in so much trouble."

"I'd have never dared do something so foolish," Lulu added. Her husband Remy kissed the back of her neck and wrapped a silvery wing around her.

Serena stopped herself before she mentioned the deer that had nearly ended Kaden McCleod's life under Lulu's watch. It wouldn't be kind and wasn't entirely Lulu's fault.

She was willing to take the punishment for her mistakes. Really though, what could Gabriel do? She'd be leaving heaven after this meeting. In fact, Lucifer was waiting just outside the office to escort her to her new home. She shivered with a mixture of trepidation and need. Aside from Lucifer, there was a veritable smorgasbord of penitents waiting for her attention, and not a single one would have a safe word.

For the first time in her life, she'd be allowed to let her dark desires run free, but she couldn't help worrying about the cost. Nothing came cheap or easy in Hell.

"Just the guardian I wanted to see," Gabriel said softly as he walked into the office. He looked relaxed and calm in a way Serena hadn't expected, given the circumstances.

"I know. I messed up this whole assignment and got caught. I wasn't aware Zinnia had intrinsic magic."

"Not quite caught." Smiling, he sat behind his desk.

"Gabriel, Zinnia caught me fair and square," Serena replied, taking the chair across the desk from him. "I made a mistake."

*Mind your own self,* indeed. It might have been funny if Serena hadn't been so appalled at her own carelessness.

"Only slightly," he corrected. "You were attempting to give her encouragement without directing her toward a specific path, exactly as the rules state."

"She still caught me. That is expressly forbidden in the commandments we created."

"Zinnia Ann Turner already believes in magic. You weren't showing her anything she didn't accept as a normal occurrence. Case in point; you did nothing to set her on the path to Vermont."

"Not true. I made sure she saw Tennyson's job offer."

"You didn't give him the idea to hire a nurse midwife, nor did you force Zinnia to accept the offer. You simply gave her the information and left it up to her to decide what to do with it."

"And you accuse us of twisting the rules to suit ourselves," she retorted, narrowing her eyes. This was completely unlike the Gabriel she knew and cheerfully despised. Guardians had been banished to

Hell for crimes of much less severity, and his reaction was both unexpected and perplexing.

Then again, she'd be able to release those poor guardians once she began her sojourn in Hell. She smiled at the thought of being a guardian for the guardians.

"She wouldn't have caught you without magic of her own." The file representing Mitchell and Zinnia burst into multicolored confetti when he tossed it into the air. Leaning back, Gabriel smirked as he watched the light show. "I actually like the new commandments. I thought I'd have to worry, but everyone is behaving themselves."

"What's your point?" Serena crossed her legs, then leaned back in her chair. "Not that it matters, since I'm leaving shortly."

"The new commandments have given me a lot of free time, and I've been thinking." Rising to his feet, he went to the door and opened it. To Serena's surprise, he invited Lucifer into his office, and she braced herself for the coming fight.

"I thought we'd already decided you were best off when you didn't think," she murmured, trying to split her attention between the two angels positioning themselves in front of her.

"Edith, Lulu, if you'll excuse us," Gabriel said,

glancing pointedly toward the door.

Lulu and Remy disappeared almost before he finished speaking, but Edith rose to her feet slowly, and only when Dimitri threatened to dump her on her ass when he stood.

"Spoilsport," she muttered. "I wanted to see the show."

"Behave, Edith," Paul said calmly, sweeping her into his arms. "Dimitri and I will give you all the show you need."

Once she was alone with Gabriel and Lucifer, she stood and crossed the office, needing some space. "All right. What are you two up to?"

"It's an interesting thing," Gabriel said, propping a hip against his desk. "It took an amoral dominatrix to convince me to have a civil conversation with my brother."

"She's not amoral," Lucifer replied, "otherwise she'd have come to me instead of you."

"And therein lies the problem." Gabriel straightened and moved to stand shoulder to shoulder with Lucifer.

Taking his brother's hand, Lucifer lifted their clenched fists. A ball of swirling sparks built around their hands, making Serena avert her eyes from the glare. Without warning, the sparks coalesced into a tightly spinning vortex and shot straight for her chest.

The force of impact drove her backward into the wall and she gasped as the searing heat of holy light burrowed into her. Flames scorched her back, burning her red suit from her body, and she screamed as wings erupted from her spine.

"What have you done to me?" She choked out the words, and fell to her knees, her hands slipping in a puddle of viscous blood. Black feathers shot with silver spread around her, stretching several feet from her body.

"Welcome to your new world order, dark angel," Lucifer said, not bothering to help her up, or even give her a robe to cover the scorched tatters of her suit.

"We're going to give Edith a present for giving us the idea," Gabriel said, crouching in front of her.

She jerked away and went sprawling, trying to ignore her lack of clothing. "What are you talking about?"

"You're going to get the best of both worlds," Lucifer said.

"We think you'll enjoy it." Gently, Gabriel helped her to her feet. "You get to remain a guardian."

"And you get to spend some time in Hell with me

doing all the things we know you really want to," Lucifer said.

Serena drew in a breath, then straightened, her body aching with remembered agony. "What's the catch?" She winced at the sharp stab of pain as she folded one wing down to cover herself. Although the feathers were velvety soft and shimmered with reflected light, the edges were razor sharp. "And what's with these wings?"

Guardian wings were always pastel colors, pale and soft, representing kindness and love. She had no idea what to think about the sharp-edged black feathers trailing to the floor and had never heard of them manifesting in such a gruesome fashion.

They were quite beautiful though, and would match her favorite Louboutin boots perfectly. Well, if she still had them, at any rate.

"We've decided to share you," Lucifer said. "I guess you could say the wings are a mixture."

"Light and dark, good and evil," Gabriel murmured, touching a feather. His fingertip welled blood that vanished almost as quickly as it appeared. "Pleasure and pain. I expect these were the wings you'd have gotten anyway because they embody your personality."

"What does that even mean?" she demanded.

"First, let's get you decent." Gabriel snapped his fingers and produced a flowing black robe.

"I'd say she's already more than decent," Lucifer murmured, giving her an appreciative gaze. Damn him, he still made her tremble like a virgin.

"What about these?" She pretended to ignore Lucifer and jerked her chin at her new appendages.

"Angel robes." Gabriel waved a hand, making the gore vanish, then laid the silk over her shoulders. To her surprise, her wings simply passed through the fabric to lay smoothly against her spine.

"Thank you." Hiding a sigh of relief, she tied the sash. "Now, someone please tell me what's going on."

"It took us weeks to figure out what to do with you," Gabriel said. "Our father is delighted we're working together."

"Well, I did have to teach you to get rid of your unfortunate streak of goodness," Lucifer added, smiling at his brother.

"And you had to learn to accept Serena's innate kindness."

"Explain. Now."

"She's still bossy," Lucifer murmured.

"I like her that way." Gabriel smiled and took a seat behind his desk. "So do you, even if you won't admit it."

"Gabriel…" She narrowed her eyes, warning filling her voice.

"Sorry. Do you remember the story of Persephone and Hades?"

"Yes, of course. What has that to do with me?"

"You'll be dividing your time," Lucifer said. "Six months up here being an insufferable do-gooder, and six months with me."

Serena folded her arms over her chest and tapped a bare foot. They couldn't possibly have resolved their differences enough to share. "You two have obviously lost your wits."

"It seemed the best way to keep you from developing a power base in either place." Gabriel tilted his head toward Lucifer and added, "Heaven doesn't want you, and Hell already knows you'll take over."

"Didn't you have that printed on a coffee cup?" Lucifer asked, smirking at her.

She tried not to smile at the memory, but nodded. Lucia had given it to her at a white elephant gift exchange party some years back. "What makes you two think I'd be interested in taking control of either place?"

They both burst out laughing and wouldn't stop, no matter how much she scowled at them. Aside from Edith, whom Serena respected, no one, living or dead, had ever laughed at her like those two irritating creatures.

"Rude!"

"Serena, love…" Lucifer coughed and wiped his streaming eyes. "I worship the ground under your adorably tiny feet, but do be serious."

Gabriel said nothing but smirked as he cut his eyes toward the framed guardian's commandments she'd helped him develop.

She studied Gabriel and Lucifer for several seconds and wondered why she was complaining. She'd be able to help that lovely cabbie, Anton, who had been so kind to Lucia, and her insides twisted with dark pleasure at the thought of tormenting the souls who rightly belonged in Hell.

"There's something you aren't telling me. What is it?"

"Why do you think that?" Lucifer asked. He examined his claws instead of looking at her.

"Do be serious," she retorted, tossing his words back at him. "If it sounds too good to be true, it probably is. You, of all people, should know that."

Gabriel sobered and nodded. "Your time will be completely divided between us. While you are here, you will not see Lucifer, nor will you perform any tormenting of the damned."

"And the opposite is true," Lucifer added. "You won't be permitted to see Gabriel or act as a guardian while you're with me."

"What happens if I don't agree?"

They gazed at her sadly, but Gabriel wouldn't meet her eyes. "Oblivion," he finally said. "I pray you don't choose it."

She shuddered, her wings flexing involuntarily as if to protect her. "That's not much of a choice, and seems overly harsh."

"It wasn't our idea," Lucifer muttered, glaring at a spot on the ceiling. "You have someone's little girl panties in a twist."

The clouds outside darkened and a bolt of lightning shot across the window. Gabriel winced and scowled at Lucifer. "Can you wait until you're back in your own realm before you insult him? I've spent a great deal of time getting my office the way I like it."

"Sorry, not sorry." Lucifer's expression softened into something almost kind, and he tugged her into a gentle hug. "Will it be so bad, do you think?"

"Given the alternative, no."

Gabriel rose to his feet and joined them. Taking her hands, he kissed her cheek. "We hoped you'd be happy. It truly would be the best of both worlds for all of us."

If she didn't accept, she'd be less than nothing. Powerless, voiceless, with no consciousness, no thought, no desire, nor even a spark to show she'd ever been a living, breathing person. Or… she could accept the offer and do everything she'd dreamed of since casting her physical body aside.

Being threatened put her back up, but one didn't thrust themselves into a coup d'état against a god because of an insult. It simply wasn't done. Her wings seemed to have a mind of their own, however, and one feather drifted down to score a deep gouge in the marble flooring.

"Gentlemen, we have a bargain."

Thank you for reading! If you enjoyed The Holiday Daddy Doms, check out Grim's Little Reaper, the first book in my new series, Club Apocalypse, available FREE at your favorite bookseller.

For sneak peeks and teasers, sign up for my newsletter. You'll also get a free book delivered right to your inbox!

# GRIM'S LITTLE REAPER

## SNEAK PEEK

ZACH

"*L*et me get this straight. You four miscreants are opening a BDSM resort together? And you want me to come to the middle of nowhere, Winslow, Arizona?"

"Yes, sir. We're calling it Club Apocalypse."

"Of course. What else would it be? And stop calling me sir."

Retirement was the devil, Captain Zach Stratton decided. He was actually considering the invitation out of sheer boredom. If nothing else, it would be good to see the Horsemen again.

RAISA GREYWOOD

Although Zach had been their commanding offi-
cer, Mark Luciano, Ryan Wood, Jake McBride, and
Sean Franklin, known respectively as War, Pestilence, Famine, and Death, had taken him under their
proverbial wing and introduced him to a world he'd
never known existed. It was the realm of pain and
delight, power and submission, and the Four
Horsemen were its lords. Despite being more than a
few years their senior, Zach was their apt pupil,
learning all they had to teach him.

"Yes, sir," Ryan said, living up to his nickname,
the pestilential bastard. "We're almost finished with
the renovation, and the pool's done."

"Are you doing the cooking?"

"Hell no! Jake is."

"Now I'm tempted." Despite Jake's nickname as
Famine, he was well-known for his uncannily
eldritch ability to make field rations palatable. What
he did with dehydrated pork patties had long been
an urban legend, still spoken of with hushed
reverence.

"He went to culinary school too. His food will
make you think you died and went to heaven, sir."

"Well, I suppose I could visit for a few days."
Zach glanced sourly around his small Grand Rapids
apartment. Aside from the largest television known

to man, there wasn't anything of note to keep him planted on his couch. "You got good scotch to go with my supper?"

"Only the best, sir."

Zach rolled his eyes and stopped himself from telling Ryan not to call him sir again. It would only make things worse. "Is the play space open for business?"

"Not yet, sir. Actually…" Zach heard a power saw firing up, then a door shut, blocking the noise. "That's the one of the reasons I'm calling. Sean remembered you liked to do woodwork, and we could use your expertise for the fixtures. We've got a contractor in, but I'd rather not have an outsider work in the dungeon."

"Ah, I see how it is. You lure me in with Jake's cooking, then expect me to work?"

"We also have a thirty-year-old bottle of Glenfiddich with your name on it, sir, and you're welcome to bring a date if you're seeing anyone."

"Bribery. Sheer bribery." Zach laughed despite himself. He'd never married, and hadn't felt like playing in a long time. The one club close to him was full of youngsters who didn't know their ass from a hole in the ground.

Then again, dominance was less about age, and

more about the willingness to listen and learn. Zach himself was a prime example.

It was a pity, really. Now that he was retired, he could explore a permanent relationship with someone. He'd seen too many broken relationships, and sadly, too many widows to risk it before, yet wondered now if he was too old for dating.

He'd met a few women who had been interested, but the relationships had fizzled when they realized they had nothing in common with him. A relationship, at least one with the kind of connection he wanted, didn't seem possible, and he wasn't interested in anonymous play partners.

"No, really. I wrote it myself in permanent marker. It says, Property of Daddy."

"Asshole. You aren't cute enough, or female enough to call me Daddy."

"Hell, sir. Even Sean knew whose bottle it is, and he likes those sweet littles as much as you do."

"So, no subs waiting for a Daddy, *and* I have to work?"

"You also get to be one of the first people to stay in one of our new suites. It has a view of… well, eventually it will be a restored desert garden with walking trails. The pool even has a Jacuzzi."

"Put a bratty sub in that room and I'll be there yesterday."

"Oh, we do have a brat," Ryan muttered. "There's a reason the landscaping isn't finished. I'd turn her over my knee myself except the parts she's completed are spectacular."

"Oh?"

"Yeah. That's the other reason we want you to visit. Jolene Miller doesn't give a good goddamn about any of us. All she wants is to restore the desert, and every time we try to fire her, she comes back like a bad penny."

"Sounds like a noble goal. Why would you try to fire her if she's doing good work?"

"She's demanding we move the parking lot to a space almost a mile away because it's blocking natural game trails. I'm done fucking with her, Zach. The woman needs a come to Jesus from someone she might actually listen to."

"Is she a redhead?" Zach asked, chuckling to himself. Ryan was probably too young to get the reference to the old Dolly Parton song.

"How did you know? Never mind. Will you come, sir? We could use your expertise. Our grand opening is in less than three weeks, and we're already booked solid."

"Bit off more than you can chew with her?"

Ryan muttered something uncomplimentary that would have gotten him court-martialed had they still been in the Navy. "She's a pain in my ass and should count herself lucky she's not my sub."

"Does she know she's working for a BDSM resort?"

"Yes, we told her that when we hired her."

"I see. Is she submissive? More importantly, does she have a partner?"

"She told us she's a widow, but we didn't ask if she had a partner. It's not our business, but I don't think she does." Ryan paused and Zach heard the sound of fingertips drumming on wood. "I suspect she might have been a sub though. She said a few things about our equipment list that make me think she's been in the lifestyle."

"Do you know her age?"

"I'd say early forties if I had to guess. Maybe a few years older than Sean."

Jolene sounded fascinating, but Zach had no intention of butting in where he wasn't wanted. "I see. And what do you expect me to do with her?"

"Sir, we might have gotten you started with kink, but you do the same magic with bratty subs that Jake does with food. You're literally the only person we could think of who Jolene might listen to, and it has to be done before she makes good on her threat to go to the press saying we're killing innocent desert creatures."

"Are you?"

"Of course not! I want the entire property restored to what it was a hundred years ago, and that includes the wildlife. I'd love to help her, but we can't give her everything she wants without going out of business before we even open."

This was an opportunity Zach couldn't pass up. He'd never been able to resist a brat, and the more he heard about Jolene Miller, the more he wanted to meet her. She sounded like the perfect challenge to bring him out of his bored funk, and he looked forward to meeting a woman close to his own age.

"I'll send you my flight information after I make my reservation. With luck, I can be there in time for supper."

## JOLENE

Humming softly, Jolene dug a small hole some yards away from the paved hiking trail. Although she wasn't a fan of concrete in a natural environment, it was necessary to make the trail accessible to guests with mobility challenges and keep everyone else from putting their big clomping feet on her plants. It had been her suggestion in the first place, and one of the few that hadn't turned into an argument with her employers, the bastards.

Jolene had grown up not thirty miles from The Majestic, now known as Club Apocalypse, and her first job had been waiting tables in the diner where the restaurant now stood. She and her late husband Ben had met there, and had even held their wedding reception in the pool area. The downward spiral for the vintage Route 66 motel had already begun before she and Ben started dating, but it had brought them together.

Ben would have been tickled to know what the new owners were doing with the place. Letting out a sigh, she tried not to think about it. He'd been gone almost five years, but she was sure he'd have talked her into purchasing a membership.

Maybe it was dumb, but she wanted to restore

The Majestic for Ben. If she made it look like it used to, she could keep hold of that small piece of him.

The Horsemen had promised her free rein to clean up the damage left by thirty years of neglect and outright maleficence. The old trailer where a meth lab blew up was the first thing to go, as was the makeshift junkyard of motorcycle parts and trash. It was far harder to repair the years' worth of ATV and dirt bike trails that had undermined the scant topsoil into a dust bowl. Unfortunately, her free rein came with enough strings to suspend even her wide ass in a Shibari tie.

She heard soft footsteps behind her and huffed out an irritable sigh. "I'm busy, Pest. You can try to fire me again later."

The footsteps stopped, and she heard an unfamiliar male chuckle that made something she hadn't felt in years twinge deep in her core.

"You aren't the first one to call him Pest."

Instead of looking up, she focused on easing the fragile endangered cactus from its nursery pot. As much as she wanted to see who had spoken, she couldn't afford a moment's inattention until she had the plant safely settled in its new home.

"I imagine that's true. Who are you and why are you here?"

"I'm here to help you."

"I thought the boys didn't have the funds to hire another landscaper." Holding the delicate cactus in a gloved hand, she carefully tapped the dirt surrounding the shallow root ball, then surrounded it with stones to keep it in place.

"They're not boys," he corrected. "And I'm not a landscaper."

"I have jeans older than they are." Knees creaking, Jolene stood and brushed the dirt off her coveralls, then turned to face the stranger.

*Well. Hello, Daddy.*

With the heavy muscularity of a real man who took care of himself, he was a touch under six feet, making it comfortable to meet his dark blue eyes surrounded by laugh lines. His gray hair was cropped short, revealing a wide forehead over a straight Roman nose. A grizzled beard couldn't quite hide the dimple in his chin.

"Zach Stratton," he said, holding out a hand.

Quickly swallowing a mouthful of drool, she got her mind off the bulge in the front of his jeans and grasped his hand firmly. She might be a middle-aged widow, but she wasn't blind and could appreciate a fine-looking man as much as the next person.

"Jolene Miller. It's a pleasure to meet you. If you'll follow me, I'll show you where I need help."

"Sir."

She stopped walking and turned to face him, hands on her hips. "Excuse me?"

"You can call me sir, although I prefer Daddy."

The bark of laughter came without warning. "Sure thing, Daddy. At least you're old enough to claim it without looking like an idiot. If you're finished with the introductions, I need you to grab a shovel and help me dig the resinbushes out from the trailhead."

"How long have you been out here?" he asked, hands still in his pockets.

"I got here at dawn. Why?"

"And water? Have you had anything to drink?"

"I'd be dead of heatstroke otherwise. Are you here to help or ask dumbass questions?"

"Well, that means you've been working around ten hours. I'm thinking it's time for baby girls to have their supper."

Jolene stared at him for several seconds, then shook her head. "Did Pest call you to force me to leave?"

He grinned, deepening the lines around his mouth. It was a good smile, warm and engaging, and she caught what might have been interested approval in his eyes as he took a step closer to brush a piece of hair off her face.

"What makes you think that?"

Despite the heat of the day, she shivered. It had been a long time since a man had touched her, and she couldn't decide if she wanted him to stop or keep going. "Let's see, you show up out of the blue, demand I call you sir, then tell me it's time to have supper. I'm thinking the boys hired you to force me to quit."

"Well, they did." He held up a hand when she opened her mouth to speak. "But I'm not going to do that."

"That makes no sense." Sweat trickled down her back, the hot desert air drying it almost as quickly as it appeared. "You know what? I don't have time for it. I have five hours of work to finish in an hour of daylight."

"I'm here to make a deal with you," he replied, moving to block her way. "You can either listen, or the Horsemen are going to call the sheriff to have you arrested for trespassing. Your choice, little girl."

Sounds like Jolene ought to make time for Zach... Grim's Little Reaper, the first book in my new series, Club Apocalypse, is available FREE at your favorite bookseller.

For sneak peeks and teasers, sign up for my newsletter. You'll also get a free book delivered right to your inbox!

# ACKNOWLEDGMENTS

As always, my undying gratitude and love go to Engineer Hubby. Without your support and faith, I wouldn't be writing at all. Love you to the moon and back, baby.

Want to see what I'm up to next? Join my Renegades on Facebook. You can also sign up for my newsletter to receive a free short story delivered right to your inbox!

## ABOUT RAISA GREYWOOD

**USA Today bestselling author of filthy smut, empty nester, and cat snuggler.**

Raisa has worked as a teacher, an actuary (her husband called her a bookie—which isn't too far from the truth), mother, and scout leader. She's happily married to her husband of twenty-seven years, and is now enjoying semi-retirement writing the books she always wanted to read with kick-ass heroines and sexy, sexy men.
www.raisagreywood.com

If paranormal romance is your jam, check out a sneak peek of Wicked Truth by her alter-ego Minette Moreau, available FREE at your favorite retailer.
www.minettemoreau.com

ALSO BY RAISA GREYWOOD

**Holiday Daddy Doms**

Jennifer's Christmas Daddy

A Valentine for Chelsea

Treats for Lucia

Zinnia's Solstice Daddy

**Club Apocalypse**

Grim's Little Reaper: A Club Apocalypse Novella

War's Peace

Pestilence's Cure

Famine's Feast

Death's Desire

Charon's Chaos

**Black Light**

Black Light: Roulette Rematch

Black Light: Saved

**Dad Bod Doms**

Henry

## Leave Me Breathless

Breaking Donatella

## Bridgewater Brides

Their Wanted Bride

## Cocky Hero Club

Sexy Scoundrel

## Standalone Titles & Anthologies

Ladder 54: Five Firefighter Romances

Masters of the Castle: Witness Protection Program

## Happily Never After (written with Sinistre Ange)

Demon Lust

Blood Lust

*T*here was a problem with barricading one's door. When her maid knocked, Lily had to get up and remove the obstacle before the woman could enter without causing a commotion.

"A moment, please, Margaret! I'll be right there!"

"Yes, ma'am. A gentleman has come to call. He says his name is Duke Denforth."

Lily tied the sash of her dressing gown and removed the barricade from the door before opening it. "Did he say what he wanted?"

Whilst Lily rarely asked for her services as a lady's maid, Margaret went straight to Lily's wardrobe, choosing the best of her day dresses. "No, ma'am. He asked to speak with your mother as well. I will try to make her presentable after I dress you."

Lily allowed Margaret to take her dressing gown and assist her into her corset and pink frock. "I don't know him. And the Denforth estate is quite a distance away, if I recall." She bit her lip, wincing when her teeth caught the edge of the scabbed cut Caine had given her. "I don't understand why a duke would call on me."

"I'm sure I don't know, ma'am. Let me do something with your hair before I tend to Mrs. Archer."

"Of course." Lily sat while Margaret brushed her hair, the blonde tresses falling to her waist in a wavy curtain. With deft movements, Margaret soon had the mass pinned into an elegant chignon. Lily's belly growled, and she laid a hand over her abdomen, knowing there would be no time for breakfast while a bloody duke sat in their parlor.

She'd forgotten her stockings, but had no time to bother with them. One didn't keep a duke waiting. Hoping he wouldn't notice, Lily settled for slippers, donning them as Margaret hurried away. Taking a deep breath, she wiped her sweaty palms on her dress and went downstairs.

As she entered the parlor, Jason Martin stood and drew her into his arms. Kissing her cheek, he said, "It's good to see you again. You look beautiful, Lily."

She grinned and hugged him tightly, so glad to see her oldest friend, aside from Elizabeth. "What are you doing here? I thought you were apprenticed to—"

"I came back to see to my brothers and met these gentlemen. They wish to make your acquaintance." Laying a hand on her arm, he kissed her once more and backed away.

A man in a somber gray suit turned away from the window to face her, and she realized he must be Duke Denforth. He looked vaguely familiar, but she couldn't place where she'd seen him. His brown hair was untidy, as if he'd been outside in a gale. His nose was straight and perfect over full lips, and his jaw had just a hint of reddish stubble. He smiled at her, flashing straight, white teeth. He wasn't particularly tall, but his carriage and bulk under the fine wool of his coat lent him quite an imposing appearance.

Two men stood with him; one dark as a midnight sky, and the other fair, with the pale complexion and red hair of an Irishman. Men with dark skin were uncommon in the countryside, and she tried to hide her avid perusal of him. The dark man's bald head and a livid scar across one cheek kept him from being conventionally handsome, but he was the most striking man she'd ever seen. Truly, both Duke Denforth's servants were arresting. The redhead appeared very young until one looked into his blue eyes. They were ancient, hard, and very cool as he caught her peeking.

Both were dressed well in bespoke suits and white shirts. They were most likely Duke Denforth's servants, and she wondered why he'd brought them to meet her.

Yet it was Denforth's eyes that caught most of her attention. She'd never seen such a startling hue before. Pale almost to translucence, the green was otherworldly. She saw dew freshened leaves in his gaze, or perhaps new spring grass. Those eyes held such wisdom, and a bit of mischief.

She dropped into a curtsy, nearly forgetting her manners. "I am very sorry to keep you waiting, Your Grace. Will you all sit? Our maid will be in with tea and scones shortly."

"Don't apologize, please. It is very early, and we have arrived unannounced. It is I who should be giving you an apology."

"Dukes don't apologize." She slapped a hand over her mouth as the redhead snorted out a laugh and her face grew hot. "I do beg your pardon. I have no idea what came over me to say such an impolite thing." Despite her embarrassment, Denforth's laughter charmed her and she smiled as he bowed, then helped her to the low chaise longue. "Will you introduce me to your companions?" she asked.

"Of course, Miss Archer." Pointing first at the mahogany-skinned man, he said, "The bald one is Moses, and the redhead who looks like he's sucked on a lemon is Liam."

They each bowed in turn, making her wonder if they were indeed servants. Both men greeted her with the clipped, modulated speech of educated gentlemen. Moses had an unfamiliar, yet charming accent. Truly, it seemed they had more appropriate manners than their master. She had better sense than to chide Duke Denforth for his poor introduction.

He settled his large body rather too close to her. She relaxed, knowing no impropriety could occur with the parlor door open and Jason in attendance. The situation was so disconcerting. Lily had no idea why he would visit her, nor did she remember ever meeting him. Why, such a man shouldn't have known of her existence, much less visited at such an unseemly hour.

Knowing she had a very short time before her

mother appeared, she gathered her nerve and asked, "Why have you come to call on me, Your Grace?"

He smiled softly, his eyes considering and thoughtful. "I will discuss it when your mother arrives. I am led to believe you don't have a male relative, so it is her to whom I will direct my inquiry."

"Yes, Your Grace. My father passed away some time ago." Lily could think of only one reason a man might make such a statement, but couldn't fathom why a duke would ask for the hand of a ruined girl with no title and a miniscule dowry, not to mention the fact that the banns had already been read for her marriage to Caine. As her friend Elizabeth had once said, marriage often involved men of middle age with bad breath and worse habits. All of those things were true of Caine Martin.

Settling back against the cushions, she hid a sigh. Duke Denforth's visit must have something to do with her late father's work. Papa had been a gifted scholar of plants and natural remedies for illness. Many of his experiments still grew in the kitchen garden and in the tiny greenhouse abutting the garden wall. Duke Denforth surely meant to purchase plants, or perhaps one of her father's books.

Truly, she was disappointed that she'd found a reasonable explanation for Denforth's presence. She'd quite liked the idea of a young and attractive duke rescuing her from the distressing fate awaiting her. She looked down at her work-worn hands and short nails. Those fanciful tales never came true except in stories, although Elizabeth seemed happy enough with her handsome earl.

When her mother tottered into the room, leaning heavily on Margaret's arm, Duke Denforth stood and helped her into the overstuffed chair in front of the fire.

Dropping a short curtsy, Margaret said, "I'll return with tea in a moment."

When the door shut behind her, Duke Denforth turned to Lily's mother, and said, "Thank you for accepting my call so early in the morning. I'm sorry to disturb you, but there is a matter I wish to discuss."

"I can't imagine what interest we would hold for you, Your Grace. My late husband had very few debts, and I'm sure they've been paid off." Grimacing, she adjusted the black scarf covering her gray hair. "Did Mr. Archer owe money to you? He did nothing aside from putter in that abysmal garden of his. He kept us fed with his tinctures, I suppose."

"No, he didn't. May I also add my condolences for your loss." He knelt in front of her chair. "I wish to contract a marriage with your daughter, Lily Archer."

Her mother barked out a laugh, sounding much like a hyena Lily had once seen at the zoo in London. "She's already engaged to the innkeeper. Besides, she's ruined for a decent marriage. As much as I love my daughter, I'm afraid that's the best she's likely to get."

"You would sentence her to a loveless marriage with a man who hits her?"

"She would have better choices had she not..." Lily's mother sighed and dabbed at her eyes with a handkerchief. "I'm afraid the matter is already done, Your Grace. She will be married to Caine Martin next week. It will be a fitting fate for a girl with loose morals."

Lily squeezed her eyes shut to stifle her tears at her mother's words, humiliated beyond anything she'd ever experienced. She'd thought her mother loved her, but Abigail Archer planned to force the marriage to punish Lily for something she hadn't done. She supposed she'd known it, but the proof of her mother's feelings toward her made her heart ache. Was she so unworthy of love and respect that even her own mother believed her to be either losing her wits or a whore? And to say such things in front of guests sent a wave of sick shame through her stomach.

Once again, she wished she'd stood up for herself all those months ago, but looking at her mother's judgmental face, she didn't think it would have helped. To her surprise, Moses and Liam moved to stand behind her, each resting a hand on her shoulders. The gesture was more comforting than she'd expected, and she wondered at their sudden attentiveness.

Duke Denforth got up and shook his head. "I'm afraid you're wrong about that, Mrs. Archer."

"I beg your pardon?"

"I am the man who was in Lily's bedchamber that night. I can also tell you that Lily is as chaste and pure as the day she was born." Turning to Lily, he added, "Even if she's been indiscreet with someone else, which I highly doubt, I don't care. Furthermore, I have enough money and power to prevent that farce of a wedding you have planned."

Her mother's face turned purple with rage and she sputtered. "You have no right to say such things to me! I am Lily's mother, and—"

Duke Denforth held up his hand, cutting off her

words. "Someone should have said them to you. Do you not see the bruises on your daughter? What happened to a mother being a safe haven for her child?"

He tossed a piece of parchment into Lily's mother's lap. "The contract with Caine Martin is dissolved, and I have a special license signed by the bishop. Miss Archer will not suffer from abuse, or your vile innuendo any longer. You may keep her damned dowry, and I'll throw in another twenty thousand to cheer your wicked soul."

Lily stood, unsure of what she intended to do. She'd always wished to see the man who had violated her so thoroughly without ever touching her, and she considered the words she'd wanted to give him.

"Excuse me."

Duke Denforth continued to trade barbs with her mother, but Lily was done listening. She got between them, facing him. "I said, shut your bloody mouths!"

She ought to be ashamed of her appalling language. It had come out almost without her control. Her angry screech brought dead, blessed silence, and she took a deep breath before addressing the rake in front of her. Margaret stood at the door to the parlor, her mouth open in shock as she wisely made herself scarce. Jason sat in his corner, a large grin on his face as he waved an encouraging hand in her direction.

"Did you just say you were the man in my room?" Lily asked.

"Yes, my dear, I will—"

"And you admit in front of witnesses that you didn't touch me?"

Taking her hand, he rubbed her knuckles. "I never laid a hand on you! Please, let me apologize—"

She pulled her hand away. "You let me suffer ruin. You let me get engaged to that foul innkeeper, and you let me debase myself entertaining Caine's filthy customers. Why do you come forth now?"

"I will explain everything after we are—"

Something energized her, a glancing touch of power that coursed through her veins. She tried to grasp it, but the energy escaped her, and she was too furious to chase it. With a scream of rage, she balled up her fist and planted a facer right to Denforth's nose.

Blood spurted and she backed away before facing her mother. "If he's still here when I return, I will accept Duke Denforth's proposal. We will be married as soon as he cleans up his face, and I will make his life a living hell for the next three hundred and thirty-two days." She stomped her foot and shook out her sore hand. "That is the precise amount of time I have suffered from his carelessness."

Both of Denforth's companions looked as if they were about to burst into laughter, and it made her even more furious, if that was possible. She pushed past them and called for Margaret to fetch Father Reynolds, then went to the kitchen to eat one of Margaret's delicious scones and swallow down a cup of tea.

She shouldn't have punched Duke Denforth. She'd been sorry for it the moment the blood gushed from his nose. And she truly didn't mean to be a shrew. He'd tried to apologize, but she'd been so angry, it was as if something had taken over her voice, making her say all those ugly words without her permission.

Guilt plagued her for her thoughts, but Lily no longer cared about her mother's opinions. It hurt that her mother thought so badly of her when she'd never done a single thing to invite her judgment. It was most likely true she would have gotten no better offer, but that didn't excuse her mother's behavior. What mother purposely pushed her only child into an abusive marriage? Even if she had done what the townspeople accused her of, there was no excuse for such treachery. Why, her mother had even said she should share Caine's bed before their wedding!

As if she would ever do such a thing. She took a deep breath to calm herself and said a prayer of thanks that her father wasn't alive to witness her mother's behavior. He'd been such a kind and gentle soul, and would be horrified by the situation. The thoughts brought a pang of sorrow. Her father would have believed her. He would have protected her.

To her surprise, Jason followed her into the kitchen and poured their tea while she fussed with the plate of scones. Setting jam and cream on the table, she asked, "Did you come to see my humiliation so you could tell your father?"

A flash of hurt darkened his brown eyes. "I followed to make sure you were all right. My father will never trouble you again," Jason replied. "I think between me and your husband-to-be, we've convinced him of the error of his ways."

She felt horrible for her unkind words. Jason wouldn't do such a thing. Laying her hand atop his, she said, "I'm sorry I said that. It was an awful thing to say. But what makes you think I should marry Denforth? By his own admission, he—"

"Came back when you needed him most, Lily." Ignoring the scones and tea, he squeezed her hand. "He's bought a special license, and left my father in a bleeding heap for you."

"I rather think you did that."

"No, I started it. Duke Denforth finished." Shuddering, he added, "I don't know that I'd have gone that far, but perhaps my father has learned his lesson."

Lily split a scone and spread jam on it. Her appetite had fled, despite her earlier hunger. "I've already said I'll marry him. I suppose we'll just have to wait and see if he stays for the wedding."

"He'll be there when you're ready," Jason said.

Why was Jason so sure of that? She couldn't join him in his faith. But perhaps being known as a termagant would be better than being known as a whore. At least this time, she'd have done what people accused her of.

MYRDDIN WIPED the blood from his face. He ignored the shrieking woman in the chair, and grinned.

What a magnificent creature his Lily was! Untaught, she'd pulled a thread of his magic away, keeping it for her own to give her enough strength to punch him. And she'd done a bloody fine job of it, to boot.

He held his handkerchief to his face and surreptitiously pushed his broken nose back into place, using a touch of magic to heal the break as Moses and Liam tried to hold back their laughter. Fates, it had been centuries since he'd seen such a powerful familiar. It was no wonder Angeline had wanted her.

"…and I cannot believe my daughter struck you! I swear to you, we brought her up better than that!"

"Do be quiet, Mrs. Archer. I deserve Lily's wrath, but she's given me a bit of a headache."

The older woman scowled, but held her peace. He thanked the heavens for small blessings as he, Moses, and Liam walked outside to wait for his bride to return.

When the door shut behind them, Liam let his laughter burst forth. "I shouldn't laugh, old friend, but the look on your face when that tiny girl punched you…" He sputtered and snorted, his giggles increasing until he had to lean against the side of the house.

"It was a surprise, to be sure," he murmured.

"You're not upset?" Moses asked, looking at him speculatively.

"No, I quite deserved her abuse." He sniffed and rubbed at his sore nose. "Although it is my hope she will keep her fists to herself after we marry."

Nodding, Moses said, "She seems a dutiful and obedient girl under normal circumstances." Wrinkling his nose, he added, "I didn't expect her to have such a sweet disposition, given her mother's appalling behavior."

When he got his laughter under control, Liam said, "I like her. She has pretty manners, and it was a delight to see her give you your comeuppance."

Myrddin sighed and shook his head. Truly, he'd been shocked at Lily's obviously uncharacteristic fit of temper. Rather than making him leery of marrying her, it only made him more intent upon having her as his wife. Despite her softness, he saw an iron will under the façade of a pale English rose. "We have something to attend to while we wait for my bride to get ready," he said.

"Oh?" Moses asked. "We'll stand with you, and you've got a ring for her. What else do we need?"

"We need to investigate her garden," Myrddin said, gesturing for them to follow as he led the way toward the blackberry bushes. "I found a nasty bit of magic in there last night that seems to siphon its health, and Lily's, too, I believe."

"Whose is it?" Liam asked, his eyes intent upon Myrddin's.

"I think it might be a stray from Angeline. She scattered magic everywhere without considering the consequences, but I didn't have time to investigate it when I was here last. Regardless," he said, walking toward the garden, "I need to make sure it's neutralized so it can't hurt anyone."

"If it was Angeline's, it will fade in good time," Moses said.

"But what if it isn't?" Liam asked.

"Once we have Lily safely in our home, I'll come back and take care of it." Yet when they reached the wall where the sick plants were, the spell had moved to another section of the garden. The plants had been pruned of blighted leaves, and when he tasted the fruit of the blackberry vine, he found it sweet. Lily's small footprints went back and forth through the beds, and he could see divots where she'd knelt to care for the injured foliage.

"The spell was here before, but now it's moved." As he pointed to the burgeoning blight on a climbing rosebush, he heard conversation from the lane and stood, cutting off his investigation when Lily's maid approached with the reverend.

He had suspicions about the nature of the foul enchantment that sickened this garden, but it didn't make sense that one of the dark Sidhe would set a spell in a place inhabited by a young woman, especially one with a small trace of light Sidhe blood. Why would the dark Sidhe bother with Lily Archer, especially when it would likely raise the ire of King Omer? King Teran of the dark Sidhe wouldn't stand for any risk to the fragile peace existing between them.

"You should ask that dragon you're carrying about," Liam whispered as the reverend walked toward the house. "He might know something."

Once Lily's maid had escorted the reverend inside, Myrddin turned to Liam. "Drako sleeps, as he has for almost a thousand years. He has no interest in conversation," Myrddin replied, unwilling to admit that he'd entertained the idea himself. However, it was always the wisest course of action to let sleeping dragons lie, even if the dragon's massive bulk rested across his shoulders.

A quietly shut door and footsteps on the gravel heralded Jason coming to join them. His lips twitched into a smile as he approached, his large hands tucked behind his back. By the time he got to the small group, he'd erased the expression from his face. But then Liam snorted, his face turning pink as he tried to hold the laughter inside.

Myrddin looked on in disgust mixed with amusement as the younger men collapsed to a marble bench next to a blooming rose bush. Leaning against each other, they laughed helplessly.

"Did you see his face?" Liam asked. "She popped his nose like a tomato!"

"We shouldn't be laughing at a duke, you know," Jason whispered.

"You're laughing, too."

"I can't help it," Jason replied, wiping his eyes with a handkerchief. "Lily is so tiny. I never realized she had it in her!" Sobering, he stood and held his hand out to Myrddin. "I believe that Lily made her displeasure quite clear, Your Grace."

"Indeed," Myrddin replied. He'd left the swelling around his nose to avoid raising suspicion. It would fade in a few hours, and he had no interest in explaining why a bloody nose had suddenly repaired itself. "She has a bit of a temper, doesn't she?"

Jason smiled fondly as he looked toward the house. "Yes," he replied. "It's astonishing because it's so rare, but when she finally explodes, it's best to get out of the way."

"I see."

Turning back to face Myrddin, his expression went flat and sober. "Her fury is nothing compared to what mine will be if I ever learn you've hurt her. I will make what we did to my father look like a Sunday stroll, and I don't give a damn if you're a duke or the Crown Prince himself."

"I have no intention of ever hurting her, Mr. Martin." Leaning closer, Myrddin asked in a soft whisper, "Did you love her that much?"

Jason shook his head. "Yes, but not as a husband should love his wife. Lily has been one of my dearest friends since childhood." He rubbed his chin and added, "Elizabeth Stratton as well, I suppose. Lily gave us both a place to hide when our parents became unmanageable."

Myrddin had no fear of the young man, of course. Despite his size, he was no match for a mage. Yet it cost him nothing to reassure Jason, and perhaps it would please his soon-to-be wife. It also gave him some insight into her character, and he wasn't unhappy with what he found. "She has a very good friend in you. I think she would be happy if you write to her, and it would be my honor to have you visit us after we're settled."

"We'll see, Your Grace." He smiled and shook his head. "I'm just a simple cooper, and I doubt I'd fit in a duke's household. But if it will please Lily, I'll visit." Glancing back at the house, his eyes lit up when he saw Lily's maid waving at them. "It looks like it's time for me to give away the bride."

Myrddin and his companions followed him back to the house. It was surprising how quickly a confirmed bachelor would jump into the parson's mousetrap for the right woman. He wondered if the young Countess Shepton would be amused by his choice. More likely, she'd be furious.

Without another word, they walked into the parlor. He stopped, his hand on the doorframe as he stared at his wife-to-be. Her honey blonde hair hung to her waist in loose curls, and was held back with ivory combs. Her blue dress was a perfect match for her spitefully glittering eyes. The capped sleeves and heart shaped bodice revealed several bruises on her pale skin, and he wanted to slit Caine Martin's throat.

Ignoring the stares and sour expressions from everyone in attendance, save himself, Liam, and Moses, he walked toward her and bowed over her hand. "I've never seen a more beautiful bride. I am honored beyond measure to call you my wife."

Will Lily forgive her handsome duke? Find out in Wicked Truth available FREE wherever ebooks are sold.

For sneak peeks and teasers, sign up for Minette's newsletter. You'll also get a free book delivered right to your inbox!